DOCTOR WHO AND THE
PLANET OF THE SPIDERS

DOCTOR WHO
AND THE PLANET
OF THE SPIDERS

Based on the BBC television serial *Doctor Who and the Planet of the Spiders* by Robert Sloman by arrangement with the British Broadcasting Corporation.

TERRANCE DICKS

A TARGET BOOK
published by
the Paperback Division of
W. H. Allen & Co. Ltd

A Target Book
Published in 1975
by the Paperback Division of W. H. Allen & Co. Ltd
A Howard & Wyndham Company
44 Hill Street, London W1X 8LB

Second impression 1978

Printed in Great Britain by
The Anchor Press Ltd, Tiptree, Essex

ISBN 0 426 10655 5

Contents

Prologue

The Mystery of the Crystal

Night falls suddenly in the rain forests of the upper Amazon. One moment, the little clearing was bathed in greenish gloom by the light filtering through the dense carpet of the tree-tops overhead; the next it was plunged into darkness.

The Indian porters were busily setting up the little encampment. Soon the tents were up, and a campfire blazing. The explorer came out of his tent, and watched the Indians going about their work, unpacking supplies and preparing the evening meal. Everything seemed normal: they had carried out this routine a hundred times before. But somehow the atmosphere was thick with fear and menace. Suddenly the men stopped work, huddled together, and began to whisper amongst themselves. The explorer thought of the heavy revolver packed somewhere at the bottom of his luggage. Then he shook his head. He wasn't going to turn against everything he'd always believed. His business was saving lives, not destroying them.

His wife came from inside the tent and joined him. She seemed tiny, almost child-like, beside his lanky form. He put out an arm and drew her to his side. She nodded towards the little group of Indians. 'They're still on the warpath, then?'

He nodded his head. 'You're telling me, love. You could cut the atmosphere with a machete.'

They stood for a moment, listening to the low voices of the Indians. Then the old man who was their recognised leader detached himself from the others and came towards the tent.

The explorer's wife looked on as the old Indian stood before them. He was speaking in a guttural, urgent voice. She had never mastered the Indian speech, but she could easily guess what he was saying. She heard her husband reply. Languages came easily to him, and he was fluent in all the Indian dialects. Perhaps it was something to do with being Welsh, she thought. After that, other languages must seem simple.

She listened intently to the voices of the two men. It was funny how much you could understand, even without knowing a word of the language. She heard the old Indian's voice, stern and insistent; then her husband's protesting, persuading. A further burst of staccato syllables from the Indian – a sweeping gesture at the blackness of the surrounding jungle that could only be a threat. Her husband again, resigned, placatory, reassuring.

The Indian peered keenly at him, black eyes impassive under the fringe of black hair. He gave a final satisfied grunt, and strode across the clearing. She could hear him talking to the others in a low voice. After a moment the porters started working again. She felt her husband's hand on her elbow, and he led her back inside the tent.

'Listen, love,' he began.

She interrupted him. 'Don't tell me – it's the crystal again, isn't it?'

He nodded. ' 'Fraid so – after that last accident at the river crossing, they're convinced it's bad luck. They've given us an ultimatum. It goes or they go.'

'But that was just an ordinary little accident.'

'We've had too many little accidents. They mean what they say.'

'Surely they wouldn't just leave us here?'

'It could be worse than that. They know they shouldn't abandon us – they'd be in trouble with the Government if we complained. So they'd probably decide it was safer to cover their tracks.'

'How?'

He took a deep breath. 'These people used to be head hunters not too long ago. They might prefer to make sure we weren't in a position to complain about them – kill us and disappear into the jungle.'

She sank down on the rickety camp bed. 'What did you say to them?'

'Well, first of all, they wanted me to throw the thing away.'

'No . . . I won't do it!' Her voice was fierce.

He raised his hand placatingly. 'Hang on – I managed to convince him that the safest thing would be to send it away. Back to where it came from, right out of their land. We'll reach one of the river trading posts day after tomorrow. You can pack it up and send it off in the mail boat. Honestly – it's the only way.'

She nodded, accepting the situation. 'O.K. I'll make up the parcel now.'

He gave her a pat on the shoulder and left the tent to supervise the porters, relieved that his wife had taken it so well. He knew how attached she was to this souvenir of her old friends and her former life.

The girl sitting on the bed sighed, and reached for the little rucksack in which she carried her personal possessions. From the bottom of it she fished a small bundle. She unwrapped it and revealed the cause of all the trouble: a many-faceted blue stone – a sort of crystal. At first, it seemed dull and opaque. Then, as you looked at it, something strange happened. Little blue fires seemed to spring up deep inside it, and the crystal began to glow. . .

She closed her eyes for a moment, and then re-wrapped the stone. She'd better send a letter with the parcel. She fished in the rucksack again, and produced a leather writing case and a ball-point pen.

Josephine Jones, formerly Jo Grant, one-time member

9

of UNIT, one-time assistant to that mysterious individual known only as the Doctor, propped the case on her knee, and began to write. . . .

Many thousands of miles away, another ex-member of UNIT crouched motionless in a darkened cellar. From his hiding place at the top of the steps, he was watching a little group of robed figures, sitting cross-legged in a circle around an intricately drawn symbol. Candles stuck into old wine bottles illuminated the weird scene with a flickering yellow light.

The men in the circle were chanting in low guttural voices, accompanying themselves with the regular clash of cymbals. They swayed to and fro as if hypnotised.

The watching man shivered in the darkness. An atmosphere of brooding evil filled the cellar, and it was growing stronger. In the centre of the chanting circle a *shape* was beginning to form . . . Near the watcher's face, a spider's web suddenly vibrated with life as the spider ran quickly to its centre. The watcher leaned forward for a better view and the silky, sticky strands of the web brushed his face. He shuddered away from their touch and jumped back, knocking over a wine bottle at his feet. Just as the chanting was rising to a peak, the bottle rolled down the steps, and smashed on the floor with an appalling crash.

The chanting stopped dead. The robed figures sprang to their feet. Some of them ran to the head of the stairs – but the watcher was gone.

Outside, in the gardens of the big old country house, Mike Yates, formerly Captain Yates, one-time member of UNIT, one-time assistant to Brigadier Lethbridge-Stewart, ran through the darkness towards his car. He was more frightened than he had ever been in his life.

The little group in the cellar had been thrown into a panic. They gathered round their leader, a middle-aged man with haggard, bitter features. His name was Lupton.

He was talking angrily to a younger, weak-faced man called Barnes, who had been sitting nearest the door. 'You're sure you didn't see anything?'

Barnes shook his head. 'It was the wind, it must have been. Blew open the cellar door, knocked the bottle over . . .' His voice tailed off, unconvincing even to himself.

'Listen,' said Lupton suddenly. 'What's that?' They heard the harsh roar of an engine going away into the distance. 'A sports car,' said Lupton menacingly. 'There's only one sports car here – it belongs to our new friend, Mr. Yates.'

I

The Menace at the Monastery

Brigadier Alastair Lethbridge-Stewart, head of the British section of UNIT, the United Nations Intelligence Taskforce, huddled deeper in his seat and hoped no one would recognise him. Not that he was engaged in some secret espionage mission; he was very much off-duty. On the other hand, you couldn't exactly say he was enjoying himself either. Why on earth he'd let the Doctor drag him to this tatty little music hall . . . The Brigadier shot a sideways glance at his companion. Elegant as always, in ruffled shirt with velvet smoking jacket, the Doctor was leaning forward with evident enjoyment.

On stage, a little man in a baggy check suit and a red nose was clutching a hand mike, leaning forward and talking very fast, as if afraid that the audience would make off before he could deliver his jokes. No one could blame them if they did, thought the Brigadier bitterly.

' 'Ere's a good one, 'eard this, 'eard this?' said the little man rapidly. 'Archimedes, you've 'eard of Archimedes, 'course you 'ave, well, when he jumped out of the bath and ran down the street with nothing on, he didn't shout "Eureka!" he shouted, "I'm a streaker!" ' The Brigadier groaned inwardly and threw the chuckling Doctor a glance of bitter reproach.

Things didn't improve much in the next hour. Act followed act, all of them pretty dreadful. The Brigadier perked up a little at the appearance of 'Fatima, exotic dancer of the Orient'. She wasn't very oriental, but she was certainly exotic, young, pretty and extremely agile.

The Doctor glanced at the Brigadier to see if this was any more to his taste. The Brigadier was leaning forward, chin in hand, an expression of intense concentration on his face. When the dance ended, and Fatima and her remaining veils undulated from the stage, the Doctor said, 'You seemed to enjoy that all right.'

'Very fit, that girl,' said the Brigadier solemnly. 'Extraordinary muscular control. Must adapt some of those movements as exercises for the men.'

The Doctor looked at him open-mouthed. 'They'd take some adapting! Surely you can't be . . . '

The Brigadier's mouth twitched under his moustache, and the Doctor realised that he was making one of his rare jokes. For once the Brigadier was pulling *his* leg. The Doctor grinned appreciatively, and pointed a long finger at the programme on his lap. 'This is what we *really* came for.'

The Brigadier peered at the programme. 'Professor Hubert Clegg,' he read. 'Mind Reader Extraordinary.'

Driving back to UNIT H.Q. half an hour later, the Brigadier still didn't feel much the wiser. The Doctor had watched Professor Clegg's act in enraptured silence, and he jumped up from his seat as soon as it was over – even though this was only the end of the first half of the show. He had stopped at the box office to leave a note for Professor Clegg before they left.

The Brigadier looked at the Doctor, who was slumped in the passenger seat deep in thought.

'I suppose you're feeling pretty disappointed, Doctor?'

'Why should I be?'

'Your Professor Clegg – didn't that performance convince you he's a fake?'

'On the contrary – it convinced me that he's a very powerful clairvoyant.'

'But that act of his was sheer trickery, Doctor,' protested the Brigadier. 'Simple word-code with his assistant. Spotted it straight away!'

The Doctor smiled. 'Oh, I know that. Now why should

a man with the powers he has use cheap tricks?'

The Brigadier was exasperated. 'How do you know he's *got* any powers?'

'Vibrations,' said the Doctor mysteriously. 'Couldn't you feel them?'

'Frankly, no.'

The Doctor rubbed his chin thoughtfully. 'I've asked Professor Clegg to visit UNIT tomorrow morning. Perhaps I can persuade him to give you a little demonstration of his real powers . . .'

Even the Doctor didn't realise that his interest in Professor Clegg was to be the prelude to the most dangerous adventure of his life.

*　　　*　　　*　　　*　　　*

Sarah Jane Smith flicked through her magazine for the tenth time, realised she wasn't taking in a single word, and threw it on the seat. She looked out of the window. The little local diesel was chugging steadily along through a very pretty rural landscape, the rolling fields stretching away on all sides. 'Very picturesque,' she thought, 'but I really shouldn't be here at all. I'm supposed to be in London, researching a story on grass-roots resistance to property speculators for that magazine.' Although Sarah was technically a free-lance, the magazine was by far her most regular source of work, and it wouldn't do to offend them. If Mike Yates hadn't sounded so desperate over the telephone . . .

It wasn't even as if she knew him all that well. They'd met during the time when London was being terrorised by prehistoric monsters brought back from the past. Yates, at this time still the Brigadier's trusted No. 2, had been tense and withdrawn. Naturally enough since, as they'd later discovered, he'd been won over to the other side and was secretly working against them. When the whole affair was finally over, Captain Yates had been diplomatically invalided out of UNIT. The official story was that he'd had some kind of nervous breakdown. No one had seen or heard of him for ages. Now here he was, popping up with some crazy story about murky goings-on in a Tibetan monastery deep in the English country-side. 'Perhaps he really *has* had a nervous breakdown,' she thought to herself, as the train jolted slowly on its way.

At that very moment, Sarah's visit was the subject of a heated argument between the man called Lupton, and a Tibetan monk whose name was Cho-Je. 'A woman journalist!' Lupton was saying angrily. 'We don't want her here.'

Cho-Je's ivory-coloured face broke into a thousand tiny, smiling wrinkles. 'We cannot shut out the world entirely, my brother,' he said in his clipped yet sing-song voice.

'That's why I *came* here to get away from the world,' said Lupton angrily. 'So did the others.'

Again Cho-Je smiled. 'One day you will learn to walk in solitude amidst all the bustle of the world.'

'It's not too late to stop her coming.'

'Oh but it is,' said Cho-Je placidly. 'Mr. Yates has already gone to meet her at the station.'

Lupton frowned. 'Yates? Did he suggest this visit?'

Cho-Je nodded. 'He knows the young lady, I believe. He brought her request to me.'

A few minutes later, Lupton was talking to Barnes in the corridor. 'How can it be coincidence?' he was saying angrily. 'He's bringing her here because he suspects some-thing.'

Barnes looked frightened. 'We'll have to stop for a while.'

'Stop – now? Just when we're on the point of breaking through? You felt the power in that circle last night – '

Lupton broke off as Tommy, the monastery handyman, shambled along the corridor. Tommy was a hulking, slow-witted youth, usually described as simple by his fellow villagers. He had worked at the monastery ever since it opened. Tommy was fiercely devoted to Cho-Je and his fellow monks – perhaps because they treated him with exactly the same quiet courtesy that they extended to everyone else.

Tommy beamed at the two men and held out a massive hand. In his palm lay a rather crumpled daisy. 'Look, pretty,' he said.

'Go and get on with your work,' said Lupton impatiently.

Tommy was indignant. 'Finished weeding. Look, Lupton, pretty flower.'

Lupton's temper snapped and he gave Tommy a savage shove. Tommy, taken by surprise, stumbled backwards and fell over his own feet. Lupton gripped Barnes by the arm and dragged him away. 'We must get the others together. There isn't much time.'

The two men disappeared down the corridor. Tommy picked himself up, groping for his precious flower, which had been squashed flat in his fall. 'Poor pretty,' he said. His face crumpled, and he began to cry.

As Mike Yates's little sports car bounced along the narrow country lane, Sarah raised her voice above the snarl of the engine. 'Let me see if I've got this straight, Mike. After you, er, left UNIT, you heard about this meditation centre, opened by these two Tibetans. You thought it might help you to get yourself sorted out, so you came down here. Now you're convinced that a group of your fellow students are up to something – but you're not sure what?'

Yates nodded. 'All sounds pretty thin, doesn't it? Maybe I shouldn't have bothered you.'

'Those men in the cellar,' said Sarah thoughtfully. 'Couldn't they just be doing some kind of special meditation?'

'Then why keep it so secret? Besides, the *atmosphere* in that cellar – it was thick with evil. You could *feel* it. I'm sure UNIT ought to know about it.'

Sarah shrugged. 'So tell the Brigadier!'

'You think he'd believe me — with my record?'

(In the cellar of the monastery, the circle of chanting figures was once more assembled. Their voices rose and fell in a guttural chant. Lupton's face was a mask of concentration. He narrowed his eyes. He could *see* the little car speeding along the narrow lane. 'Now,' he muttered hoarsely. 'Now . . .')

Sarah frowned and shook her head. A sudden sense of oppression, of dread, was coming over her. She felt a sudden irrational impulse to beg Mike to turn back. She told herself not to be silly and said, 'So you want me to take a look around, and then report to the Brig for you?'

Yates nodded. She could read the appeal in his eyes. Sarah said dubiously, 'Well, all right, Mike. But I'll need quite a bit of convincing before I go to the Brig with some daft story about mad monks . . .'

(In the cellar the chanting rose to a peak. 'Now!' said Lupton fiercely. 'Now!')

The sports car was tearing down a country lane. Although still narrow, the lane ran in a straight line for a mile ahead of them. It was now completely empty, and Mike had instinctively put his foot down.

The tractor just *couldn't* have been there. The lane was empty; there were no turnings or gates. Yet suddenly it *was* there, its huge red bulk blocking the entire lane as they rushed towards it.

Mike wrenched the wheel round and shot the sports car through a gap in the hedge. They burst through into a field, the car skidded round in a huge arc, back through a second gap, and on to the road again. With a shrieking of brakes, it skidded to a halt.

Mike Yates sat very still, gripping the wheel so hard that it hurt his hands. He drew a deep breath and turned to Sarah. She was looking over her shoulder, back at the tractor – but there *was* no tractor. It had vanished, as impossibly as it had appeared. The lane was empty.

Sarah said shakily, 'You saw it too, Mike?'

'The tractor? Yes, of course.'

Sarah's face was grim. 'All right, Mike. I'm convinced. Let's visit this monastery of yours.'

2

The Deadly Experiment

Off-stage, Professor Clegg looked shabby, and rather insignificant. The 'artistic' bow-tie was faded, the black velvet smoking jacket long past its former elegance. But the Professor held himself upright, and did his best to put a good face on things. He swept off his battered hat with a flourish, and said jauntily, 'Gentlemen! A very great pleasure to meet you.'

The Brigadier nodded a little stiffly, but the Doctor replied with equally formal courtesy 'Professor Clegg! It was extremely kind of you to come.'

Once the social preliminaries were over, the Professor felt rather at a loss. 'As a matter of fact, I'm not sure why I *have* come. Your message *was* a little ambiguous.' He looked at the Brigadier's uniformed figure, and hazarded a guess. 'You want me to do my act for you? A regimental guest night, perhaps? I do quite a deal of cabaret work.'

'Good lord, no!' said the Brigadier hastily. Then, realising he'd been a little too hasty for politeness, he added, 'Clever stuff mind you, but not really my cup of tea.'

The Doctor cut in hurriedly, 'As a matter of fact, Professor, I asked you to come here because I'm doing a little research into E.S.P.'

'That's extra sensory perception, you know,' said the Brigadier helpfully.

Clegg smiled. 'Oh yes. As a matter of fact, I do know.'

The Brigadier looked a little deflated. 'Well, I didn't. Not till the Doctor explained.'

The Doctor gave Clegg a reassuring smile. 'You see, I'm trying to cover the whole field – psychometry, clairvoyance, telepathy, and so on. I very much hope you can help me, Professor.'

Clegg began to look frightened. He edged nervously towards the door. 'I'm sorry, I'm afraid I can't. You see, to begin with, I'm not a professor at all. That's just for stage purposes. And as for my act . . .'

'All a lot of tricks, eh?' said the Brigadier knowingly. 'Word-code with your assistant, that sort of thing?'

Clegg nodded dumbly. The Brigadier shot the Doctor an 'I told you so' look. The Doctor said gently, 'Don't worry, Professor Clegg, your secret in safe with me – your real secret, that is.' He paused for a moment, and said deliberately, 'I shall tell no one that you really *do* have super-normal powers.'

Clegg seemed to deflate, like a punctured balloon. He reeled as if about to faint, and sank down gratefully into a chair pushed forward by the Brigadier.

'It's true, isn't it?' said the Doctor.

Clegg nodded. 'It's happening more and more,' he whispered. 'I don't *want* it. I was quite happy just as a performer. Now I seem to be developing this power. I hate it. The things I can do! They frighten me.'

'Do?' said the Doctor keenly. 'Do you mean teleportation?'

'Well, no. But psychokinesis, yes.'

Despite his newly-acquired knowledge of the paranormal, the Brigadier was now out of his depth. He shot the Doctor an enquiring glance. 'Psycho what?'

'Psychokinesis,' said the Doctor impatiently. 'Moving objects by the power of the mind. Professor-Mr.-Clegg, do you think we might have a demonstration?'

Clegg looked dubious. 'Well . . . ' he said unenthusiastically.

The Doctor gave him a most charming smile. 'Please try. It would be of the greatest assistance to me.'

Clegg braced himself, then nodded. 'Very well.' He

glanced round the laboratory. The Doctor and the Brigadier had been having coffee just before his arrival, and the tray with the coffee things still stood on one of the laboratory benches. Clegg stared at it fixedly and with a frown of concentration. The Doctor and the Brigadier followed the direction of his gaze. Suddenly, the tray rose a few feet into the air. It hovered uncertainly for a moment and floated into the middle of the room. Then Clegg gasped, 'I can't . . . I can't . . . ' He rubbed his hand across his eyes and the tray crashed to the ground.

The Brigadier jumped. 'Jolly impressive,' he said a little nervously. 'You ought to use that in your act.'

Clegg rounded on him fiercely. 'And lose my sanity? It would be a poor exchange.' The little man was white and sweating, his face drained with effort.

The Doctor put a reassuring hand on his shoulder. 'Mr. Clegg, your powers are perfectly normal. They lie dormant in everyone.'

Clegg sighed. 'If only I could believe that. I feel such a – a freak.'

'Help me in my experiments,' said the Doctor urgently. 'We can learn more about your powers, help you to control them. We can find others like you, so that you won't be so alone . . . '

Clegg looked up at him, new hope in his eyes. 'If you can do that, Doctor,' he said eagerly, 'you'll make my life worth living again. Of course I'll help you as much as I can.'

'Splendid!' said the Doctor. 'We'll get started right away, shall we?' Before Clegg could reply, the Doctor wheeled forward a trolley bearing a load of intimidating electronic equipment. The main feature was a metallic helmet, rather like an ultra-modern ladies' hair-drier. It was supported by an extensible arm, and linked to a series of dials. Briskly the Doctor whisked the contraption behind Clegg's chair and popped the helmet on his head.

The Brigadier looked on in total bafflement,

'What is all that stuff, Doctor?'

'Oh, I've designed one or two bits of equipment,' the Doctor explained airily. 'This is my improved version of the electro-encephalograph. It'll measure his brainwaves as we carry out the tests.' He turned to Clegg, who was cowering nervously under the helmet. 'Shall we try a little simple psychometry? Perhaps you'd lend Mr. Clegg your watch, Brigadier?'

If the Brigadier had any doubts about Clegg's powers, they were finally disposed of in the next few minutes. Holding the watch in his hands, Clegg closed his eyes and said slowly, 'This watch was given to you a few years ago . . . somewhere by the sea. Brighton, was it? A young lady called Doris . . .'

Very embarrassed by this reminder of his days as a gay young subaltern, the Brigadier almost snatched the watch back. 'All true!' he said hurriedly. 'Absolutely spot on.' He shot the Doctor an appealing glance. 'Surely you've got enough, Doctor?'

The Doctor chuckled. 'A little too much, eh, Alastair?' He made further adjustments to the electronic jumble on the trolley, this time linking the metal helmet to a little screen, rather like a mini TV set. 'This is my IRIS machine, Mr. Clegg. Image Reproduction Integrating System. It will translate your thoughts into pictures on this screen. Now, try this.'

The Doctor handed Clegg a strange device. It was shaped like a very slim torch, with numerous mysterious attachments. This was the Doctor's trusty sonic screwdriver, a multi-purpose tool that had been his companion on many adventures.

Clegg held the little device in his hands. A flood of terrifying images rushed into his mind. On the little TV screen patterns began to swirl . . . The head of a terrifying monster swam up, roaring ferociously, gnashing row upon row of jagged teeth. Clegg gasped and let go of the sonic screwdriver. The Doctor reached out a long arm and caught the screwdriver as it dropped from the man's fingers. Clegg gasped. 'That thing . . . what was it?'

'A Drashig!' said the Doctor happily. 'The most ferocious omnivore in the cosmos. Don't worry, Mr. Clegg, you're doing very well. But perhaps we'd better find you a less alarming subject . . .'

As if on cue, Sergeant Benton entered the laboratory. He was carrying a small parcel. He saluted the Brigadier, and then looked with interest at the figure of Clegg sitting under the metal helmet. 'Going in for a bit of hairdressing, Doctor?' he asked amiably. Catching the Brigadier's warning frown, he went on hurriedly, 'Parcel just arrived, sir. Thought it might be urgent.'

'For the Doctor, or for me?' snapped the Brigadier.

'For all of us, sir, in a way. It's addressed to the Doctor, *or* Brigadier Lethbridge-Stewart, or Captain Yates, or Sergeant Benton!'

The Doctor was making further adjustments to the tangle of his electronic equipment. 'Open it!' he suggested. Then he straightened up. 'No, wait a moment.' He took the parcel from Benton and handed it to Clegg.

'See what you can do with this, my dear chap.'

Clegg took the parcel and turned it over and over in his hands. On the IRIS screen the image of a strange, alien landscape began to form.

'This has come a long way,' said Clegg slowly. 'From beyond the stars . . . a meteorite . . . no it's a gemstone . . . a blue jewel!'

'Of course!' said the Doctor. He took the parcel from Clegg and tore off the wrappings to reveal a battered cardboard box. He lifted the lid and found a folded letter. Beneath it, resting in a bed of cotton wool, lay the blue crystal from Metebelis Three.

Jo's parcel had arrived.

*   *   *   *   *

Sarah Jane Smith was beginning to wonder if she had been wasting her time after all. Shortly after the mysteriously vanishing tractor had so nearly caused the crash, Mike Yates had driven her to a big old country mansion set in rambling, overgrown grounds. He had introduced her to a beaming little monk called Cho-Je, who had discoursed to her at some lengths on such subjects as 'the fullness of the void' and 'the emptiness of the ten thousand things'. Sarah hadn't understood a word of it, and had said so. With an infectious giggle, Cho-Je had said delightedly, 'Quite right! The Dharma that can be spoken is no true Dharma!' and had packed her off with Mike Yates for a tour of the meditation centre.

Mike had shown her the big hushed library, with its rows upon rows of esoteric books. She had visited the simple meditation rooms, where little groups of men sat cross-legged, sometimes in complete silence, and sometimes chanting softly. 'What are they meditating about?' she had asked.

Mike had given her a pitying look. 'Not *about* anything. They're just . . . meditating. It's an exercise in awareness!'

Having apparently seen everything there was to see, Mike was now leading her along a corridor at the back of the house. He looked at his watch. 'Come on. Time we hid ourselves in the cellar.'

'Good,' said Sarah, hoping they were at last reaching the purpose of her visit. Certainly, she'd seen nothing sinister so far. Indeed, the child-like happiness of Cho-Je had impressed her enormously, though she was as far as ever from grasping how he'd attained it.

They turned a corner and ran slap into two men. The one in front, a middle-aged man, was wearing a shabby sports coat. He had a haggard, bitter face. A younger, weak-looking man hovered behind him. Sarah shivered involuntarily. Could these be their unknown enemies?

Lupton gave them a thin smile. 'Good afternoon, my brother.' He raised his eyebrows enquiringly at Sarah. Suddenly Yates found himself on the defensive.

'This is Miss Smith,' he said. 'From a London magazine. Sarah, meet Mr. Lupton and Mr. Barnes.'

Lupton nodded condescendingly. 'Cho-Je told me you

were coming. I trust you have had a pleasant visit?'

Sarah decided she didn't care for Mr. Lupton. She didn't like his appearance, or his manner. 'Yes thank you,' she said. Then she added in a deliberately challenging tone, 'After a very bad start.'

Lupton gave her a look of supercilious enquiry that verged on a sneer. 'Indeed?'

'We had an accident,' Sarah went on. 'We were nearly killed.'

'You were lucky to escape,' said Lupton coldly. 'The roads round here can be *very* dangerous for visitors. Very dangerous indeed.' The threatening tone was unmistakable. 'Won't you have a cup of tea before you go?'

Yates grabbed Sarah by the arm. 'I'm afraid Miss Smith has to leave now, or she'll miss her train back to London.'

Sarah refused to budge. 'Nonsense, there's plenty of time.'

'I rather think you must have misread the time-table,' said Yates firmly. He took Sarah's arm and almost dragged her away.

Lupton watched them go. He smiled bitterly. 'You know, Barnes, I don't think we'll have any more trouble. That girl could have been dangerous – but our friend Mr. Yates is scared out of his wits. Call the others – we carry on as planned.'

Barnes nodded and hurried off.

In Mike Yates' car, Sarah was protesting vigorously. 'You say you want me to see for myself, then we just take off. What's going on?'

Mike started the engine and drove slowly out of the front gates.

'Look, Sarah, Lupton *knew* you were coming down. He must have been responsible for that tractor hallucination.'

Sarah looked at him in exasperation. 'I'm sure he was. But why should we let him scare us off?'

25

'We're letting him *think* he's scared us off,' Yates corrected her. 'Now we double back on foot.'

Sarah grinned. 'Ah, the fiendish cunning of the man!' she said admiringly.

Yates turned left and left again, cut off the engine, and coasted down the lane that ran round the back of the house. The car drew up silently, close to the high wall that surrounded the grounds. Yates stepped on to the bonnet, and climbed on to the top of the wall. He extended a helping hand to Sarah so that she could follow him. They dropped down inside the grounds, and Yates led her through a tangle of shrubbery to a back window. He clambered through, and Sarah followed him.

As she struggled through the little window and into the corridor, the shadow of a hulking form fell over her. She gasped, but Yates squeezed her arm reassuringly. 'Hullo, Tommy,' he said. Sarah saw a massive young man in old corduroys and a shaggy roll-neck sweater. For all his size and obvious strength, his round blue eyes held the simple curiosity of a child.

'Why you climbing in window?' he grunted.

Yates looked at him in consternation. Tommy was quite unpredictable. He might well raise a hullaballoo that would wreck everything.

'Playing a game?' asked Tommy.

Yates nodded. 'That's right, Tommy. Just a game!'

'Tommy likes games. I'll play too.' He looked at them hopefully. Mike gave Sarah a despairing glance.

'The thing is, Tommy,' said Sarah confidingly, 'the name of the game is "Secrets". It's a secret that we're here. You won't tell anyone, will you?'

Tommy shook his head. His eye was attracted by the sparkle of Sarah's brooch. He reached out to touch it, and Sarah said gently, 'Would you like it?' Tommy nodded eagerly, and Sarah took off the brooch and handed it to him. Delighted, Tommy grabbed it from her, and wandered off down the corridor, totally absorbed in his new prize.

'A shameless display of feminine wiles!' said Mike. 'Come on.'

As they approached the cellar, they could hear the sound of low, rhythmic chanting. Mike opened the heavy wooden door, took Sarah's arm and guided her into the darkness. Just inside was the little landing where he had hidden before. She gasped as something brushed across her face. 'Ugh! It's thick with spiders' webs!'

'Sssh!' said Mike urgently. Cautiously they peered round the turn of the wall.

A circle of robed figures was seated round an ornate symbol, a sort of silken poster which lay flat on the cellar floor. She whispered in Mike's ear. 'What's that they're sitting round?'

'It's called a mandala – a device for focussing their concentration.'

In the gloom of the cellar, Sarah could see Lupton leading the chanting, with Barnes beside him. She had seen most of the other men in her tour round the monastery. The chanting was quickening its pace now, building up a strange sense of foreboding. Sarah blinked. An unearthly glow was spreading from the mandala in the centre of the circle. A sense of dread began to flood over her. Something evil was happening in the cellar, something she didn't want to see. She felt an urge to run, but the chanting held her in a hypnotic spell.

At exactly this time, the Doctor was finishing the letter that had come with the parcel. He was reading it out to the Brigadier and Sergeant Benton. ' . . . and the Indian porters are saying it's bad medicine – like *it* goes or *they* go!' The Doctor frowned, reflecting that neither Jo's grammar nor her handwriting had improved since she left UNIT. He struggled to make out the hastily scrawled final paragraph. 'So, Doctor, if you're away on a cheap day trip to Mars or something, perhaps *you* could look after it for me; or you, Brigadier, if you're whooping it up in Geneva; or what about you, my lovely Sergeant Benton?'

Benton, who had been suppressing a grin at the reference to his two superiors, blushed beneath his tan. The Brigadier's lips twitched under his moustache, and the Doctor puzzled over the last sentence . . .

All three had forgotten Clegg, who, during the reading of the long and rambling letter, had been sitting meekly underneath the metal helmet. They hadn't noticed when he had reached out and picked up the crystal, peering curiously into its blue depths.

Suddenly Clegg went rigid. He felt some tremendously powerful force flooding into the room, a force that was somehow working *through* the blue crystal in his hands.

'Must go now or I'll miss the next cleft stick to civilisation,' the Doctor read slowly. Suddenly an invisible force swept through the room. The letter was plucked from the Doctor's hand and swept up to the ceiling as if caught in a powerful up-draught. It was followed by almost everything else portable in the laboratory. Chairs, tables, equipment, all swirled up in the air in a mad whirlpool. The Doctor, Brigadier and Benton were flung across the room. Clegg sat in his chair, motionless in the swirling chaos around him.

The mad whirlpool of objects suddenly stopped. Things crashed to the floor, many of them smashing. The Doctor looked round. The laboratory was a shambles. Benton and the Brigadier were staggering to their feet. The Doctor looked at Clegg, still sitting in his chair. 'Mr. Clegg, are you alright?'

There was no reply. The Doctor came closer. The little man was hunched forward in his chair, gazing into the crystal. His face held an expression of unutterable horror . He was quite dead.

In the cellar of the monastery, the chanting reached a climax. Sarah was gripping Mike's arm hard enough to bruise it, though neither one of them was aware of the fact. The strange glow around the mandala seemed to condense and solidify. A shape was forming. Sarah blinked again, trying not to believe her eyes. But it was *there*, it was true. Crouching on the mandala was an enormous spider . . .

3

The Coming of the Spider

For a moment, the Spider crouched motionless on the mandala. Lupton and his circle were paralysed with terror. One man leaped to his feet and ran for the steps. A strand of almost invisible white light snaked out from the Spider's body. As it touched the fleeing man, he convulsed and dropped to the floor.

The Spider seemed to swing to and fro, as if scanning the circle of men. No one dared to move. Lupton sat frozen with the others, struggling to regain control of his will. The forbidden books that he had stolen from Cho-Je's library had warned that misuse of the Rituals of Power could summon up demons. In his eagerness for wealth and success, he had ignored the warnings. Now it seemed that he was to pay the price of his rashness. He searched his mind desperately for one of the Incantations of Banishment. Finally, he assembled the words in his mind. Moistening his lips he managed to croak out an incantation that should have sent the creature back from whence it came. It had absolutely no effect. Instead, Lupton felt an icy tendril of thought reaching out to touch his mind. Then the Spider spoke to him. Not out loud, of course, but inside his head. Her voice – somehow Lupton knew that the creature was female – was clear, sweet and icily evil . . .

'Lupton! I have come to give you the power you seek. Why do you try to send me away? Turn around.'

Wincing from the alien intruder in his mind, Lupton

didn't move. The Spider spoke again, her voice sharp and commanding. 'Turn around, I say.'

Slowly Lupton turned his back. To their horror, those in the circle saw the Spider quiver for a moment and then spring at Lupton's back. For a moment it seemed to cling between his shoulder blades, then it vanished.

Lupton stood stooped for a moment. Then he straightened up and turned round. His voice was calm and authoritative. 'All of you – go back to your rooms. You will say nothing of what has happened here.'

Barnes indicated the man crumpled at the foot of the cellar steps. 'What about him? Is he dead?'

Lupton shook his head. 'He is simply unconscious. Take him to his room. He will wake soon and remember nothing.'

Obedient to the authority in Lupton's voice, some of the little group began to lift the body.

Meanwhile, Mike Yates and Sarah were hurrying along the corridor. 'Hadn't you better come away with me?' Sarah was asking.

Mike shook his head. 'It's better if you go by yourself. I'll stay and keep an eye on things here. You let the Doctor and the Brigadier know what's going on.'

'But, Mike – I don't *know* what's going on.'

They reached the window by which they had entered, and Mike opened it so Sarah could climb out. 'Just tell them everything you saw.'

'What are you going to do?'

'I'm going to try and see the Abbot, tell him all about it. Now, off you go! Here – take my car.' He handed her the keys.

Sarah saw he was determined. 'All right, Mike, I'm going. Take care of yourself.'

She disappeared out of the window, and Mike closed it behind her.

For a moment he hesitated, wondering what to do next. Should he tackle the Abbot right away? No, better wait. Lupton and his lot might still be on the prowl.

Just before bedtime when everything was quiet, that would be the best time . . . Suddenly he heard voices coming towards him – Lupton and Barnes! Hurriedly, Mike made off in the opposite direction.

Barnes was still desperately trying to get some kind of sense out of his friend and leader. Lupton seemed full of a vast, unshakable confidence. He talked airily of the most grandiose plans, of wealth and power unlimited, in the tones of one who held the world in the palm of his hand.

Barnes was a good deal less happy. 'But that spider,' he persisted. 'What was it? One of those Tibetan demons the books warned us about?'

Lupton smiled. 'No doubt our friend Cho-Je would say that. But he would be wrong.'

'Where did it go?'

'My dear Barnes, it didn't *go* anywhere. It's still here!'

'You can feel it – on your back?'

'Not on my back. In my mind. I can hear it speak to me.'

Inside Lupton's head, the icy voice said, 'This man is stupid – send him away.'

Barnes saw Lupton's eyes close in concentration, and asked, 'Was it speaking to you then? What did it say?'

'It said you looked tired. You should go to your room and rest. That's what I'm going to do.'

Lupton patted Barnes on the shoulder and urged him towards the stairs. 'Now don't worry. I *know* what I'm doing . . .'

*   *   *   *   *

Later that same evening, Benton moved slowly about the laboratory, setting things back in place. The Doctor was sitting on a stool, gazing bleakly into the distance. Benton understood that the death of the Professor had hit him hard.

The Brigadier came in and said briskly, 'Packed off

that police chappy at last. According to the post mortem, it was a natural death. Poor chap had a weak heart.'

'Perhaps he did,' said the Doctor grimly, 'but I'm still responsible, you know. I gave him the crystal to look at – and something he saw while he was holding it gave him such a shock that his heart gave out. It killed him.'

'The same something that turned the place upside down,' said Benton.

The Doctor nodded. 'A tremendous explosion of psychokinetic force . . . Wait a moment – there's just a chance . . . '

The Brigadier felt very irritated by all this mystery. 'A chance of *what*, Doctor?'

The Doctor was busily sorting out his tangle of electronic equipment, now back on its trolley. 'He was still attached to the IRIS machine when he died. It should have recorded his thoughts for us – if it hasn't been shaken up too badly.' The Doctor turned the machine on and adjusted the controls. It gave out a high-pitched electronic noise, like a tape being wound backwards at high speed. The Doctor twiddled a bit more, and blurred pictures began to form on the little screen. The Brigadier peered over the Doctor's shoulder, trying to make sense of the distorted shapes : shapes with round furry bodies, and many legs. 'Bless my soul,' said the Brigadier, 'looks like a lot of . . . '

'Spiders!' said the Doctor. 'Now why should the crystal have made the poor chap think of spiders?' He stood brooding for a moment, then said decisively, 'Only one thing to do – I shall have to look into the crystal for myself.'

Benton and the Brigadier both started to protest.

'Far too dangerous,' snapped the Brigadier.

'Let me have a go,' said Benton.

The Doctor ignored them. 'Don't you see? A man's dead, and I'm responsible. The least I can do is find out what happened, and why.' He reached for the crystal and then paused – 'There *is* one thing you could do for me,

Sergeant Benton. I'd just love another cup of your excellent coffee.'

With a worried glance at the Brigadier, Benton hurried from the laboratory. The Doctor picked up the blue crystal and put it on the bench before him. Climbing back on to his stool, he rested his elbows on the bench, his chin in his hands, and gazed into the crystal's shimmering blue depths. The Brigadier looked on uneasily, pacing about the laboratory. The Doctor sat motionless. The silence stretched on and on until the Brigadier couldn't stand the suspense any longer. He cleared his throat noisily. 'Any luck, Doctor?'

No answer. The Brigadier came closer, and peered at the Doctor cautiously. He was still hunched over the crystal. He wasn't moving. As far as the Brigadier could see, he wasn't even *breathing*. Blue flames seemed to dance and flicker in the heart of the blue jewel . . .

*　　*　　*　　*　　*

Lupton lay day-dreaming on his bed, hands behind his head. His mind was full of the wealth and power that would soon be his. *How* exactly this was to come about he was not quite sure. But it *would* happen. The Spider had promised. Suddenly an agonising mental pang jerked him into full consciousness. He spoke to the unseen being in his mind. 'What is it?'

'The crystal. I can *feel* it. Concentrate, Lupton. Concentrate!'

'What crystal?'

The cold voice vibrated with urgency. 'That is why I have come. To find the crystal and get it back. It will give us power. The power we both seek. Concentrate!'

Lupton's face twisted with effort as the Spider joined her mind to his.

'I see a man,' he said slowly. 'A man gazing into a blue jewel . . . A man they call the Doctor . . . '

*　　*　　*　　*　　*

'Doctor!' said the Brigadier urgently. Then again, louder, 'Doctor!' The Doctor didn't so much as twitch. Benton hurried in with a tray holding three steaming coffee mugs. He put the tray down on the bench, close to the Doctor.

'Here we are, Doctor – coffee up.'

'No use talking to *him*,' said the Brigadier. 'Looks as if we've got an emergency on our hands. Damn silly thing to do, said so all along. I'd better get the Medical Officer.' He picked up the internal phone, dialled, and said, 'Dr Sweetman – get over here to the laboratory right away –'

'Sir – look!' whispered Benton urgently.

A wisp of steam from one of the coffee mugs was floating up under the Doctor's nose. And the nose was twitching! Suddenly, the Doctor blinked, reached for a coffee mug, took a long swig and said, 'Delicious! You know, Sergeant Benton, next to Mrs. Samuel Pepys, you make the best cup of coffee I've ever tasted.' He took another swig.

The Brigadier snapped into the phone. 'Never mind, Dr Sweetman, the emergency seems to be over.' He slammed the receiver down and said, 'Now, Doctor, never mind the dratted coffee, what about the crystal? Did you see spiders, too?'

The Doctor shook his head. He rose, stretched and went over to the window.

'When I was young,' he said, as if continuing a previous conversation, 'an old hermit lived half-way up a mountain behind our house. It was from him that I first learnt to look into my own mind.'

The Brigadier seemed singularly unimpressed by this reminiscence. 'What did you see in the crystal, Doctor?'

'That's what I'm trying to *tell* you. I saw the face of my old teacher.' The Doctor turned, and his voice was very serious. 'Do you know, Brigadier, I've got a feeling I'm about to be faced with the worst threat, the greatest danger, of my entire life. It was as if that old hermit was reaching out across the years to help me . . . '

*　　*　　*　　*　　*

Outside the door of the Abbot's private suite, Mike Yates was arguing with Cho-Je – and finding it a hopeless task. 'See K'anpo Rimpoche?' The little monk was scandalised. 'No, no, of _course_ not. You know our Abbot is in seclusion. He sees no one.'

'But it's very important,' Yates protested.

'Nothing is important, Mr. Yates, except to strive,' Cho-Je giggled disconcertingly, 'for enlightment, that is. As for this spider demon you think you have seen, many strange things will appear to you in meditation. You must – what is the word – salute them and walk on. Go to bed, Mr. Yates!'

Cho-Je smiled benignly and disappeared down the corridor. As soon as the little monk was out of sight, Yates reached determinedly for the Abbot's door. A massive form loomed up behind him, and a huge hairy paw grasped his wrist. It was Tommy.

'Cho-Je say go to bed, Yates.'

'Listen, Tommy, I've _got_ to talk to K'anpo.'

'K'anpo Tommy's friend. He like to be alone. Go to bed. I fetch Cho-Je – or I hit you.'

Tommy raised an enormous fist, and Yates stepped back. 'All right, Tommy.'

The fist was lowered and Tommy looked pleased. 'Good. I don't like to hit you.' He settled his huge shoulders against the Abbot's door, obviously a fixture for the night.

Yates sighed and walked away. There didn't seem to be very much he could do. Cho-Je wouldn't listen, and he'd never reach the Abbot without clobbering Tommy, which seemed a bit extreme even if he could manage it. Deciding to live to fight another day, Yates headed for his room, hoping Sarah would have better luck in

36

convincing the Doctor. As he started up the main stair-case, he met Lupton coming down.

Yates looked at him curiously. Lupton seemed in a state of exaltation. His eyes were glittering.

'Time for all good little boys to go to bed, eh, Mr. Yates?'

'What about you?'

'Just a little constitutional. Goodnight, Mr. Yates.'

Mike Yates climbed the stairs to bed, and Lupton walked out of the front door. As he made for his car, he could still hear the cold clear voice inside his head. 'Hurry, Lupton, we must find the man with the crystal. We must find him and take it from him!'

'Suppose he doesn't want to part with it?'

The Spider's voice was matter of fact. 'Nothing matters except the crystal. If the Doctor resists us, you must kill him.'

4

The Chase for the Crystal

When Sarah called on the Doctor early next morning, she found him hard at work in his laboratory. On one of the benches, he had rigged up a riot of wires and condensers, connected at one end to a little monitor screen, and at the other to the blue crystal from Metebelis Three.

Thinking over the baffling events of the previous day, the Doctor had realised first that the crystal was somehow at the centre of things, and second that he didn't know nearly enough about it. He'd taken the crystal from Metebelis to study it, having searched carefully for a jewel with exactly the right characteristics. But although he had sometimes made use of the crystal's strange powers, he had never really investigated it properly. On a sudden impulse, he had given it to Jo Grant for her wedding present, she had taken it to South America, and then he'd forgotten all about it.

Now, eager to make up for lost time, the Doctor was subjecting the crystal to a full electronic analysis, with the aid of one of his own inimitable lash-ups of improvised scientific equipment.

Eagerly, Sarah poured out the whole story of her trip to the monastery. The Doctor appeared to be listening keenly, nodding his head intelligently from time to time, and encouraging her to continue with occasional 'ums' and 'ahs'. She came to the end of her story, and looked at him expectantly. 'Fascinating!' he said. 'Absolutely fascinating!'

Sarah smiled, pleased that the Doctor didn't think

she'd been wasting his time. The Doctor looked up at her and said solemnly, 'The crystal lattice is absolutely balanced, right and left.'

Sarah groaned, realising he hadn't heard a single word of her story. The Doctor looked at her, puzzled because she didn't seem to share his pleasure. 'It's a scientific pun,' he explained. 'Coherent thought !'

'Doctor ! What *about* this man Lupton? What about this giant spider that jumped on his back and vanished?'

The Doctor stared vacantly at her for a moment and then said thoughtfully :

'It's probably analagous to the laser . . . ' He bent over his apparatus and adjusted controls. Blue sparks flickered round the crystal, and a complicated pattern of wave-traces flickered across the screen.

Sarah glared at his back, tempted to crown him with one of his own bunsen burners. Suddenly, the Doctor looked up at her and said urgently, 'Spiders? Did you say spiders?? *Giant* spiders?'

Sarah nodded weakly,

The Doctor came up to her and put his hands on her shoulders, his face very grave. 'Now, Sarah,' he said solemnly, 'I want you to tell me the whole story, right from the beginning.'

Sarah sighed, and started all over again. 'Well, I got this call from Mike Yates – he was down at this meditation centre place . . . '

Corporal Hodges, Unit Transport Section, gave the Doctor's new car a wipe with a damp cloth, and stepped back to admire his work. He always enjoyed looking after the Doctor's personal transport. Like the Doctor himself, it had character. First there had been Bessie, the old Edwardian roadster with the amazing turn of speed. Now there was this new car. Well, you couldn't exactly call it a *car*. More like a cross between a flying saucer and a hovercraft.

Reflected in the gleaming surface of the vehicle, Hodges saw someone coming towards him. It was a stranger, a middle-aged man in a shabby sports jacket.

'He's got a nerve,' thought Hodges, 'walking in as if he owned the place.'

Although UNIT was a semi-secret organisation, Hodges nevertheless wasn't particularly alarmed or surprised. No attempt had been made to disguise the fact that the H.Q. was a military establishment of *some* kind. Getting into the outer areas was comparatively easy. Access to the inner security area was impossible – unless you had the right credentials.

Hodges straightened up as the man approached. 'Can I help you, sir?'

The man stopped. 'I'm looking for the Doctor.'

'Dr Sweetman, sir? The Medical Officer?'

The man paused. It seemed almost as if he were listening to some inner voice.

'No . . . ' he said slowly, 'the – other Doctor.'

'Ah, the Scientific Adviser.' That explained it, thought Hodges. All sorts of weird people turned up to see the Doctor. 'You'll find him through that door over there, sir. Turn left and left again when you get inside.'

The man nodded his thanks and moved away. Hodges said, 'Excuse me, sir!'

The man stopped. He glared at Hodges impatiently. 'Well?'

'Could I see your pass please, sir?'

'Pass?'

'Can't go into the Central buildings without a pass. Didn't they give you one at the main gate?'

'Oh yes. Yes, of course.' The man reached for his pocket. Suddenly he stretched out his hand in a curious pointing gesture. A thread of fire snaked from his finger-tips, and blasted Hodges into unconsciousness. Lupton turned and ran for the door into the main building.

'So you see,' the Doctor was saying, 'poor Professor Clegg saw spiders before he died, and you saw spiders at the monastery. There *must* be a connection. And it *has* to be this crystal!'

Sarah looked at the blue gem, sitting incongruously amongst the tangle of electronic equipment. 'Where did it come from anyway?'

'I brought it back some time ago, from a planet called Metebelis Three.'

Briefly, the Doctor told Sarah the history of the jewel, and of its strange power to affect the mind.

'You mean it could, well, drive someone mad?'

'Just the opposite. It clears the mind, and amplifies its powers.'

'But it *could* be used for evil purposes?'

'Oh yes. If the minds using it were motivated by evil . . . '

Sarah shivered. 'The minds of the giant spiders on Metebelis Three?'

'That's just it,' said the Doctor. 'There aren't any.'

In the corridors nearby, Lupton moved cautiously on his way. 'Nearer,' said the voice of the Spider inside his head. 'We are getting closer – we are almost there.' Following its directions, Lupton came nearer and nearer to the Doctor's laboratory. Suddenly, a big man in army uniform came round the corner and stood in front of him.

'Excuse me, sir, you're in a security area. May I see your pass?'

Lupton ignored him, and went on. Sergeant Benton was outraged. Automatically, he drew his revolver. 'Halt, or I fire!' Lupton swung round and stretched out his hand. Benton was slammed to the ground by what felt like a massive electric shock, and Lupton ran on.

'Land squids with great hairy tentacles,' the Doctor said. 'Giant snakes, an eagle the size of a house . . . but no spiders. In fact, no really intelligent life at all.' The Doctor rubbed his chin. 'Wait a minute, though – there could be a time difference!'

As an old friend of the Doctor, Sarah took the concept of time travel for granted. 'You mean the spiders come from an earlier period than the time of your visit?'

'That's right. Or a later one.'

Unseen by the Doctor or Sarah, a face appeared at the glass partition dividing the laboratory from the corridor. It was Lupton. He could see the crystal glowing on the laboratory bench. It was almost within his grasp.

'It's there,' he whispered. 'A blue crystal. It *must* be the one!'

'Concentrate!' said the Spider's voice inside his head. 'You must concentrate.'

The Doctor and Sarah were looking at the crystal too. 'Let's assume there *are* intelligent giant spiders on Metebelis Three,' said the Doctor matter-of-factly. 'Then why is there all this activity? Unless . . .'

'Unless what?'

'Unless,' said the Doctor slowly, 'they want the crystal back . . .'

As he spoke, the crystal vanished before their eyes.

In fact, it hadn't travelled very far. It was resting in the palm of Lupton's hand just a few feet away, snatched there by the Spider's power of teleportation. Lupton was looking at it in incredulous triumph, when Benton staggered round the corner.

Thanks to his size and strength, he had recovered from the Spider's blast far quicker than most men could have done. But he was still a little shaky. Quickly, Lupton shoved him aside, and hurried past. Benton took a wild shot, but missed by several yards. He was just about to set off in pursuit when the Doctor and Sarah shot out of the laboratory. The Doctor grabbed him by the shoulder, steadying him. 'What happened, old chap?'

'Some bloke – stranger,' gasped Benton. 'He's got your crystal! Come on.'

All three set off in pursuit.

Lupton ran back through the door by which he had entered the building. He was half-way across the car-park and heading for the gate by the time the Doctor, Sarah and Benton reached the same door. To the Doctor's delight, he saw the Brigadier turn in through the gate. The Doctor cupped his hands and bellowed, 'Brigadier! Stop that man!'

Confused but willing, the Brigadier drew his revolver and yelled, 'Halt!'

He fired a warning shot over Lupton's head. Lupton skidded to a stop. He turned to go back, only to see the Doctor, Benton and Sarah heading towards him.

Automatically, he raised his hand, expecting the Spider to give him the power to blast them down. But the voice inside his head said, 'No! They are too many and too distant. We *must* escape.'

Lupton looked round wildly. The big car park was full of army vehicles of all kinds; landrovers, motor-bikes, a staff car, even a little one-man helicopter. The nearest, and the fastest-looking, was a low, almost circular vehicle which resembled an ultra-modern racing car. Lupton sprinted to it, pulled back the entrance hatch, and jumped in.

The Doctor, to his vast indignation, saw his pride and joy, his new experimental car, being driven out of the gates. The Brigadier had to jump aside as the strange-looking vehicle whizzed past him. Automatically he raised his revolver to shoot at the tyres, and then realised that the blessed thing hadn't got any tyres! The Doctor said in an anguished voice, 'Don't shoot, Brigadier, you'll damage my new car!'

Sarah and Benton came speeding up to the gate in Bessie. The Doctor glanced round the car-park. He indicated the little helicopter. 'You three get after him in Bessie. I'll spot him from the air and guide you.'

The little group broke up. The Doctor ran for the helicopter, and the Brigadier with a crisp, 'Move over, Benton,' got behind the wheel of Bessie. The little roadster shot off after Lupton.

The Doctor swung his long legs into the cockpit of the

little helicopter. Looking like a large, unwieldy dragon-fly, it took off with a shattering roar, and was soon climbing steeply over the UNIT car-park.

The Doctor looked down at the countryside beneath, the roads spread out like a map. He soon spotted his stolen car, and the bright yellow shape of Bessie in hot pursuit. From the Doctor's vantage point it was clear that the newer vehicle was slowly drawing ahead. Poor old Bessie just hadn't got the power. The Doctor flipped the switch of his intercom. 'Hullo, Brigadier, is this thing working? Can you hear me?'

The Brigadier's voice crackled back. 'Loud and clear, Doctor. We're on his tail.'

'Yes, but he's getting away from you. Take the next right fork and you'll be able to cut him off.'

A Police Panda car was tucked into the side of the little country lane. The driver was having a quiet doze before returning to the hurly-burly of the main road. Suddenly he jerked awake as two very odd-looking vehicles flashed past. He grabbed his radio-mike, too shaken to observe correct procedure. 'Listen, there's a sort of silver hover-craft being chased by an old crock. They're both doing about ninety!' The policeman instinctively ducked, as something whirred over his head, then added to his message. 'And there's a little tiny helicopter after 'em both. I'm in pursuit. Over.'

The flat voice of the base radio operator droned in reply, 'Thank you, X-ray Tango. Your message is timed at —' Suddenly the voice broke off, became human. 'Oy! *What* did you say?' But the policeman was too busy driving to reply.

The Brigadier took the next right fork, as the Doctor had suggested, but Lupton's extra speed was just too much for them. The silvery shape whizzed past their bonnet before they could cut him off. The Brigadier cursed, muttered an apology to Sarah — who was clinging petrified to Benton's arm — swung the car round, and set off again after Lupton. By now their quarry was out of sight, but soon the Doctor's voice crackled in their ears. 'He's about half a mile in front of you. He's turned off to the left.'

The chase went on. For all her old-fashioned appearance, Bessie was capable of an amazing turn of speed. But the Doctor's newest creation, with its more powerful engine and streamlined shape, was just too much for her. Thanks to the Doctor's spotting from overhead, they never entirely *lost* heir quarry, but it was getting increasingly obvious that they didn't have very much chance of *catching* him either.

Lupton, crouched behind the padded wheel of the Doctor's car, soon made the connection between the maddening persistence of his followers and the helicopter which buzzed overhead. What he needed was cover. He made for the open ground ahead of him. Perhaps one of those clumps of trees . . .

A few minutes later, Bessie bumped across a patch of rough heathland and drew up beside the Doctor's stolen car. It was parked, empty, at the edge of a patch of woodland. The Brigadier stood up in Bessie's front seat, and looked around him. Lupton was nowhere to be seen. 'Pretty cunning move,' thought the Brigadier. 'While he was driving that car of the Doctor's we could *see* him even if we couldn't catch him. But an ordinary looking man in everyday clothes is much harder to find. Let the fellow reach any sort of town and he'll disappear like a piece of straw in a haystack.'

There came a roar from overhead, and a sudden fierce wind, as the Doctor touched down in his little helicopter. He leaped out of the cockpit and raced across to them. 'Gone!' said the Brigadier with a sweeping gesture at the rough country that surrounded them.

'So he has,' said the Doctor. 'We'll just have to look for him!'

'I'll rustle up a patrol,' said the Brigadier. 'He won't have got far.'

(The Brigadier's words were truer than he realised.

45

Lupton was crouched, still as a rabbit, in a fold of ground not very far away. His old brown sports jacket blended almost perfectly with his surroundings.)

They heard the sound of another car engine, and a police car jolted across the heath towards them. The policeman got out, and produced his notebook. The people were as peculiar as the vehicles, he thought. A full-blown general (or something), a bloke in fancy dress, with a trendy-looking bird. In a voice of official severity the policeman said, 'I'll thank you all for a few particulars. You were touching ninety back there . . .'

From his hiding place, Lupton peered out at the little group. They were arguing with the policeman, everyone apparently talking at once. 'This is the diversion we need,' said the icy voice inside Lupton's head. 'We can escape in the flying vehicle.'

'But I don't know how to fly it.'

'I will guide your hands,' said the Spider. 'Come!'

The Brigadier had placated angry Prime Ministers in his time, but an English policeman in hot pursuit of a motoring offence was beyond his powers. 'Alastair Lethbridge-Stewart, eh?' said the policeman in tones that indicated he suspected it of being an alias. 'Would you mind spelling that, sir?'

It was Sarah who spotted Lupton as he broke from cover and dashed for the helicopter. 'Hey,' she yelled, tugging the Doctor's sleeve. Immediately the policeman found himself with no one to question, as they all ran to try and head off Lupton. The Doctor was in the lead, but as he reached out to grab the door Lupton slammed it shut, and the helicopter became airborne with a shattering roar. The blast of the take-off bowled the Doctor over, and by the time he was on his feet again Lupton was climbing steeply. Soon he was no more than a dot in the sky.

The Doctor started running towards the futuristic-looking craft that Lupton had first stolen. Sarah was close behind him and, as he leaped into the driving seat, she scrambled into the passenger seat beside him. 'You're not going without me, Doctor,' she said, before he could protest.

The Doctor grinned, his face alight with the joy of the chase. 'Suit yourself,' he yelled, and closed the hatch over their heads. 'Fasten your safety belt!' The car sped away across the heath.

From her seat beside the Doctor, Sarah looked down at the ground rushing away beneath them. She wondered how they could go so fast and so smoothly over such rough terrain. Suddenly she realised that the ground really *was* beneath them, and was receding more and more . . . 'Doctor,' she yelled, 'we're flying!'

The Doctor concentrated his attention on the wealth of controls set into the crowded dashboard in front of him – controls, Sarah realised, which looked far more suited to the cockpit of a jet plane than to any car. 'Well of course we're flying,' he said reasonably. 'How are we going to catch him if we don't?'

Notebook limp in his hand, the policeman stood gaping as the silvery shape disappeared into the sky like the flying saucer it so much resembled. He turned to demand an explanation, but the two soldiers were already back inside the tatty old roadster, shooting off into the distance. The policeman sighed. He walked back to his car on legs that felt suddenly a little wobbly. He picked up the radio mike and said, 'X-ray Tango to control. Can I come in please? I don't feel very well.'

Lupton sat at the controls feeling like a kind of automatic pilot. His hands seemed to know exactly what to do, even though the brain that controlled them was not his own. He began to relax a little, confident that they had shaken off the Doctor. Suddenly, a silver shape swept down from the sky above and buzzed him, missing, it seemed, by inches.

The Doctor gave Sarah an exultant smile and said, 'That gave him a turn! Came down at him out of the sun. The Red Baron was very fond of that particular trick.' The Doctor's long fingers flicked over the controls, and their craft seemed to hover over the little helicopter. 'He'll have to land soon,' said the Doctor confidently. 'He must be almost out of fuel. Those things don't hold much.'

Suddenly Lupton became aware of an ugly change in the engine note. One of the dials in front of him was flickering to zero. 'We're out of fuel!' he yelled.

'Land,' ordered the Spider, 'there by the water.' Below them stretched the estuary of a biggish river, which wound its way across the countryside. Lupton felt his hand move over the controls, and the ground came suddenly nearer.

Hovering above him, the Doctor said, 'You see, he's landing.' He started to glide down in pursuit of the helicopter. From her window, Sarah saw the helicopter land by the sprawling buildings of a boat yard. Lupton jumped to the ground and dodged out of sight. The Doctor landed his craft close to the helicopter. He and Sarah jumped out. 'Wait here,' snapped the Doctor. Before Sarah could protest, he set off after Lupton on foot.

Bob Armitage, the owner of the boat yard, was mooring his motorboat at the landing stage, congratulating himself on a well-spent morning. Recently he'd taken the gamble of ordering a line of one-man hovercraft, and at this very moment Mr. Pemberthy, a wealthy local resident, was completing a test run. Bob was sure from the man's reaction that the sale was in the bag. Sure enough, a moment later, Pemberthy steered the little hovercraft up to the landing stage, his face wreathed in smiles. 'Fantastic, Bob! Wish I could buy a dozen of 'em. As it is, I'll have to make do with one!'

Bob finished mooring his motorboat, and took the line that Pemberthy threw him from the hovercraft. As he started to make it fast, a man dashed out from nowhere, shoved him clean off the jetty and into the water, and jumped into the motorboat. Bob disappeared into the river with a colossal splash. The astonished Pemberthy climbed out of the hovercraft and prepared to grapple with the intruder. But the stranger raised his hand in a pointing gesture, and Pemberthy was blasted from the jetty. Bob Armitage, now treading water, swam over to the unconscious Pemberthy, grabbed him and started pulling him ashore. The motorboat roared away upstream.

A second man, tall and white-haired, came running along the jetty, jumped into the hovercraft, and roared away after the motorboat.

The Doctor spared a moment from his pursuit of Lupton to appreciate the hovercraft: nice, nippy little thing, a pleasure to drive. He wondered if he could talk the Brigadier into getting one for UNIT. Bound to come in useful.

He rounded a bend in the twisting river, and saw Lupton speeding away in front of him. The Doctor realised that the conditions of the chase were now reversed. Lupton had the larger, more powerful transport, and the Doctor had to rely on superior skill to give him a chance of catching up. Lupton was drawing steadily ahead. Soon he would be out of sight, able to abandon the motorboat, and make off inland.

Suddenly, the Doctor grinned. The river in front of them wound to and fro in a series of S-bends. Lupton had to follow those bends. But the Doctor didn't! He was in a hovercraft. Land and water were all the same to him. The Doctor swung the little hovercraft up the bank, across the road, over a field (and, quite without realising it, over a very astonished sleeping tramp) and back on to the river. By cutting off the bend, he had gained a considerable distance. Now he was right on Lupton's tail.

Behind the wheel of the powerful boat, Lupton was filled with despair. The man wasn't human. Would he never give up? 'He'll catch us!' he told his unseen companion. The Spider's voice was as icily calm as ever. 'Then I will summon help. I must contact the source of power. Help me. Concentrate.'

The Doctor repeated his land-hopping manoeuvre, this time giving a homeward-bound herd of cows a very nasty shock. He cut off another bend, gained even more distance and emerged back on the river, level with Lupton's boat. The two craft veered towards each other on a collision course. The Doctor saw that Lupton wasn't even steering. He crouched in the motorboat, gripping the wheel and staring ahead like a man in a trance. The Doctor brought his hovercraft alongside, matched speeds, and took a flying leap . . . He landed in the back of Lupton's boat, staggered, and recovered his balance. He turned to grapple with Lupton — but there *was* no Lupton. No one was manning the controls; no one swam or floated in the water nearby: Lupton had vanished.

5

The Council of the Spiders

Lupton was almost as surprised as the Doctor. One moment, capture seemed certain. He had been in the motorboat, desperately gripping the wheel. He could see the Doctor jumping towards him from the hovercraft. Then everything went blank and he once more stood in the familiar corridor of the monastery, stone flagstones beneath his feet.

Lupton reeled, holding a hand out to the wall to support himself. He looked round to get his bearings. He was just by the back stairs, close to the cellar. He blinked incredulously. It was real. It was true. He *had* escaped! A sudden thought struck him. He reached in his jacket pocket and took out the crystal. The blue jewel sparkled in a shaft of sunlight from a nearby window. Lupton smiled to himself, replaced the jewel in his pocket, and hurried towards his room.

The door to the old cupboard under the stairs opened a crack, and Tommy peeped out. He rubbed a massive hand over his forehead. His face wrinkled with the effort of thought. It wasn't so much Lupton's popping up from nowhere that bothered him. Most things in life were a mystery to Tommy, and nearly everyone seemed to have powers he couldn't master – things like reading and writing. No, it was the blue jewel. He had never seen anything so beautiful in his life. He *had* to have it . . . Moving silently, for all his size, Tommy followed Lupton down the corridor.

As Lupton was about to enter his room, Cho-Je passed him with a smile and a nod. Lupton forced himself to smile back, and hurriedly opened the door. Safely inside, he took the crystal from his pocket and put it on the dressing-table. It sparkled in the morning sunlight. 'We've done it,' he said exultantly. 'Will it really give us power?'

Inside his head the voice said, 'More power than you have ever dreamed of.'

Even the icy tones of the Spider seemed tinged with triumph, then she spoke again, sharply this time. 'Veil your mind, Lupton. Conceal your ambitions. If my sisters on Metebelis Three could read your desires, they would kill you.'

It was Lupton's first indication that the Spiders were not all united in their aims. Before he could ask more questions, a strange, high-pitched humming seemed to fill the room. He staggered and collapsed on the bed.

'Beware,' said the Spider's voice. 'They seek to make the link. Veil your mind!'

Lupton felt the room blur and dissolve around him. His surroundings vanished. Not suddenly, as when the Spider had teleported him from the motorboat to the monastery, but slowly, swimmingly. Yet all the time Lupton was aware that this was not a *real* transformation. His body was still resting on the bed in his room. Only his mind had moved. It was being drawn through endless voids of space, away, away ...

Suddenly Lupton seemed to be in – a place. Not a room or a cave, but a vast gloomy hollow, criss-crossed with cobwebby strands. In sudden terror, he realised that he was at the heart of a giant web. Ranged in front of him he saw row upon row of giant spiders. Their thin, clear voices set up a continuous high-pitched humming, causing the strands of the web to vibrate. He was in the Council Chamber of the Spiders, Rulers of Metebelis Three. They were all grouped in a semi-circle round one particular Spider, larger and more powerful than all the rest. Somehow Lupton knew that this was the Spider Queen. Her voice, when she spoke, crackled with authority. 'You were successful?'

Lupton heard *his* Spider, the one inside his head, answer, 'Totally. The crystal is ours.' A hum of approval went up from the Spider Council.

The Queen said, 'You have done well. Prepare to return, bringing the crystal with you. It will take time to build up the power. When we are ready the two-legs must perform the ritual that concentrates his mind.'

Lupton sensed that to these creatures he was no more than a fly caught in their webs. He made an effort and forced himself to speak. 'And what about *me*? You need *me* to make the link, to bring the crystal back. Without *me* you wouldn't have recovered your precious crystal at all. I have been your friend. I must be rewarded!'

A gasp of horror went up from the Council. 'A two-legs dares to claim friendship with the eight-legs, the Noble Ones?' said the Queen in horror.

Lupton would have spoken again but *his* Spider intervened. 'Forgive him, O Queen,' she said placatingly. 'He means no harm, and he *has* served us well.'

Another Spider spoke. 'Then his reward shall be to serve us further. We shall use him in the great work, the conquest of Earth. That is the secret purpose of the Council.'

The Council Chamber began to dissolve around him. Dimly, he heard the Queen's voice saying, 'We have exhausted our power. Be ready, be ready . . .'

Suddenly he was back in his room, on his bed. He sat up gasping, but the Spider spoke soothingly inside his head. 'Rest now. Let the power return to your body and to your mind. Rest, Lupton.' Slowly he drifted into sleep, rolling over, face downwards, his head pillowed in his arms.

After a moment the giant Spider materialised, sitting on his back. It hopped from the bed, scuttled towards the door and vanished . . .

Some time later a quaint old Edwardian roadster drove

up to the monastery. Two visitors got out, a tall white-haired man and a young girl. The tall man insisted on seeing Cho-Je, and when it became apparent that he wasn't going away until he did, Cho-Je agreed to receive them. They sat in the hall. Students drifted in and out, others sat quietly reading or meditating.

Sarah listened as the Doctor gave Cho-Je a brief account of the theft of the crystal, and their reasons for visiting him.

The little monk waited until the Doctor had finished, without showing the slightest sign of surprise or disbelief. 'Most interesting, Doctor,' he said blandly, 'but I assure you it is impossible that Mr. Lupton had any connection with these strange events.' Lupton's friend Barnes, who had been sitting nearby, slipped quietly out of the room. Scarcely had he gone when the Spider materialised behind the door. She crouched, listening.

'But it *was* Lupton,' Sarah was protesting. 'I *saw* him. I recognised him.'

Cho-Je gave his most infuriating smile. 'Doctor, you say you . . . ah . . . lost sight of Mr. Lupton at about half-past ten? On a river over a hundred miles from here?'

The Doctor nodded.

'At exactly half-past ten, I was on my way to the Meditation Class. I passed Mr. Lupton as he was going into his room. We greeted each other. Now, unless he was transported here in the twinkling of an eye . . .'

'Stranger things have happened,' said the Doctor levelly.

Cho-Je nodded solemnly. 'As we know, such things are child's play to a true Master. But you surely cannot believe that Mr. Lupton possesses such powers. He is still a novice.'

Lupton surfaced angrily from a deeply refreshing sleep, filled with dreams of vast, undefined power. He realised

54

that Barnes was shaking him, and snarled. 'What is it?'

Barnes' voice was panicky. 'That girl – she's come back. There's someone called the Doctor with her. They say you stole some kind of jewel . . .' Barnes' eyes widened as he saw the blue gem sitting incongruously on the dressing-table next to Lupton's hairbrush. 'Then it's true!' he whispered.

Lupton got to his feet. He felt confident, strong. Without answering he went to the little wash basin, took off his jacket, and splashed his face with water.

He waited until he had towelled himself dry before he spoke, 'Do you know why I came here?' Barnes shook his head. 'Right! Potted history coming up.' There was a savage bitterness in Lupton's voice.

He sat on the bed, gazing into the past, 'Picture me: bright young salesman, sales manager, finally sales director. I gave them twenty-five years of my life. Then the take-over boys moved in. Golden handshake for poor old Lupton. So – I set up on my own. You know what happened? The big boys broke me. Very efficiently, too. I'm still looking for some of the bits.'

(Sunk in his memories Lupton didn't see Tommy's face appear at the open window. Tommy saw the jewel gleaming on the dressing-table. He stretched out an arm, scooped it up, and disappeared from sight.)

Barnes said, puzzled, 'So you came here to seek peace of mind?'

Lupton roared with laughter. 'I came here for power! I want to see *them* grovelling to *me*. I want to see *them* eating dirt.'

Barnes looked at him in horror, shaken by the venom in Lupton's voice. 'You mean you want to take over the firm that ruined you – something like that?'

'More than that, Barnes. I just might take over the whole stinking world.'

Looking guiltily over his shoulder, Tommy slipped into the cupboard under the back stairs. No one ever came here – it was his own special hideaway. He switched on the cupboard light, blinking in the harsh glare from the naked bulb. Buried under a pile of junk in one corner was an old cardboard shoe-box – Tommy's treasure chest. He took off the lid to reveal a collection of odds and ends : pieces of glass, brightly-coloured stones, odds and ends of broken, worthless jewellery – anything that sparkled and shone enough to appeal to Tommy's magpie instinct. The brooch that Sarah had given him rested on top of the collection. Next to it Tommy carefully laid the blue crystal from Metebelis Three. He put the lid back on the box, returned it to its hiding place, switched out the light and slipped back into the corridor, an expression of innocence on his face.

Lupton was just putting his jacket back on when he saw Barnes's face fill with horror. Barnes pointed a shaking finger. By the door, the Spider crouched looking at them. Lupton said, 'You'd better go, Barnes.' Thankfully, Barnes slipped out of the room.

The Spider said, 'Lupton, the one called the Doctor is here. You will go and see him, lull his suspicions.'

Lupton said, 'Don't be ridiculous. He knows me. He saw me. He's too dangerous to trifle with. I intend to keep out of his way.'

Lupton felt a lash of cold rage from the Spider's mind. She was not used to disobedience. A sudden wave of psychic pain washed through his brain. His face twisted in agony. Yet somehow Lupton knew that he could endure the pain. He could master it. He could even . . . send . . . it . . . back! Lupton's face twisted with effort and suddenly the Spider began to thrash convulsively on the floor. 'No, Lupton, no ! Stop – please !'

Lupton's face relaxed, and the Spider became still. Struggling to recover her strength, she said, 'You are strong, Lupton, stronger and cleverer than the two-legs of Metebelis Three.'

'I'm cleverer than most of them on Earth,' said Lupton. 'And I've no intention of becoming a slave to you, or that arrogant Queen of yours.'

56

'I like her arrogance no more than you, Lupton. You seek power on Earth, I on Metebelis. We must help each other.'

Lupton smiled. He could feel that she was trying to recover his good will. 'Very well – but as an equal partnership. Remember that!'

He turned, and the Spider leaped on to his back, and disappeared. He heard her voice inside his head. 'Now – the crystal. Soon we must leave.'

Lupton turned to the dressing-table. The crystal was gone.

In the hall, Mike Yates and Sarah were listening to the duel of words between the Doctor and Cho-Je. Each of the two men was calm, polite and utterly determined. Under the unassuming exterior of the little monk, the Doctor could feel an intelligence and will that was a match for his own.

'May we *see* this man, Lupton?' said the Doctor. 'I'm sorry to be so pressing, but it really is extremely urgent!'

'In the West,' said Cho-Je infuriatingly, 'you whip your poor horse too much. He is exhausted, and yet he never leaves his stable . . .'

The Doctor smiled, acknowledging the truth of Cho-Je's argument. 'That is very true – and yet has it not also been said . . .' Dropping into sonorous Tibetan, the Doctor countered with a text from one of the more obscure Tibetan masters.

Yates and Sarah gave each other despairing looks. Tommy slipped into the hall and beckoned to Sarah from the doorway. Unnoticed by the Doctor and Cho-Je, who were exchanging Tibetan texts like two small boys comparing stamp collections, Sarah moved towards the door. Tommy tugged at her sleeve and said, 'Sarah, come with me. Tommy got present for you.'

'Well, not now I'm afraid, Tommy.'

Tommy tightened his grip. 'Please – you come now.'

57

Sarah sighed. She might as well go off with Tommy as sit here listening to the Doctor and Cho-Je chatting away in Tibetan. 'All right,' she said. She moved to Mike Yates and indicated that she was going off with Tommy, and wouldn't be long.

Mike waved back, and then turned his attention to the Doctor and Cho-Je.

They had reverted to English, though for all he could understand of their conversation they might as well have gone on talking Tibetan.

'There is only the Now,' Cho-Je was saying happily. 'The Here and the Now, the present moment with no duration – which is Eternity!'

'But time is the element we are born into,' countered the Doctor. 'We swim in it like a fish in a bowl of water.'

Cho-Je chuckled. 'Yet how much happier that fish would be if you tipped the bowl of water into the ocean . . .'

'Or better still,' said the Doctor solemnly, 'tipped the ocean into the bowl!'

The Doctor and Cho-Je laughed uproariously. 'I suppose it'll all mean something to me one day,' thought Mike. Then to his relief, he saw the Doctor rise to his feet. Calmly the Doctor said, 'And *now* may we see Mr. Lupton?'

Cho-Je smiled. He had taken a mischievous delight in verbal fencing with the Doctor, but he knew when he was beaten. 'But of course,' he said, as though the issue had never been in doubt. 'Mr. Moss, will you please find Mr. Lupton for this gentleman?' Moss, a small bearded man, nodded obediently and set off.

Lupton was pacing his room. 'You must give me time. I'll find the crystal. Someone's taken it.'

'There is no time,' said the Spider, her voice filled with fear. 'My sisters are building the power now. I can feel it. Soon they will be ready to take us back to Metebelis.'

'And if we refuse to go?'

'They will use that power to blast us out of existence!

I shall die, and you will lose your mind!'

Lupton shuddered. 'And if we go without the crystal . . .'

'If the Queen learns on our arrival that we have lost the crystal, she will kill us both in her rage.'

Lupton paused, then he nodded decisively. 'We'll bluff them. We'll pretend we've still got it. We have no choice.' He went to a cupboard and produced the mandala. With the silken cloth rolled under his arm, he left his room and hurried towards the cellar. If he used the back stairs he could get there without being seen.

Sarah followed Tommy along the corridors to the door of his special cupboard. 'You wait here,' he said mysteriously, and disappeared inside. Sarah shrugged and waited. After a moment, she heard footsteps coming towards her.

Reluctant to explain why she was hanging about, Sarah ducked inside Tommy's cupboard. Tommy, who was fumbling with a shoe-box, looked up at her suspiciously. 'Someone's coming,' she explained. 'Ssh!' Satisfied that she wasn't spying out his hiding place, Tommy nodded obediently. Sarah had left the cupboard door a little ajar, and, with idle curiosity, she peeped out.

To her surprise, she saw Lupton hurrying along the corridor, the mandala cloth tucked under his arm. He looked round, then went through the door to the cellar. She waited till he was out of sight and turned to Tommy. 'Listen, Tommy, you know Mike Yates in the great hall?' Tommy nodded.

'Tell him Lupton's gone into the cellar,' whispered Sarah urgently. 'Say I'm going down there, too.' She slipped back into the corridor, leaving Tommy clutching the shoe-box.

He called after her. 'Sarah — I got present for you.' But she was gone. Sadly, Tommy opened his shoe-box and looked at the blue crystal, gleaming on top of his pile of treasures. Still, he could always give it to her later. He put the box back in hiding and stood thinking.

Now what was it she'd asked him to do? Something to do with Mr. Yates...

As Sarah crept down the cellar steps a strange feeling came over her that all this had happened before. But this time there was no little group of robed figures: only Lupton, cross-legged before the mandala, his voice rising and falling in a strange guttural chant. Just as before, she could feel the surge of power building up. Lupton's voice rose and fell, and a strange glow began to appear around the mandala. She wondered if more spiders would arrive...

In the hall, Moss was reporting to Cho-Je, 'Honestly, I've looked *everywhere*. Not in his room, not meditating. Maybe he's gone for a walk.' Tommy's bulky form loomed up, dwarfing Moss.

'Hey, Yates,' he called loudly.

'Not now, Tommy,' said Yates.

Tommy was indignant. 'You want Lupton — he's in cellar. Sarah too. She followed him!'

The Doctor was instantly on the alert. 'Where is this cellar, Mike?'

Yates was already moving. 'This way, Doctor. I'll show you.' The Doctor ran after him.

In the cellar, Lupton's chanting reached a sudden peak. He stepped on to the glowing mandala — and vanished. Instinctively Sarah got to her feet and ran down the steps. There was still a faint glow around the intricate design. Somehow it seemed to *draw* her. Slowly, as if hypnotised, Sarah put first one foot and then the other on to the mandala.

She heard a shout from the head of the cellar steps. It was the Doctor, Yates at his side. The Doctor called, 'Sarah — step back. Get off that thing!'

She tried to obey but she couldn't. She felt herself being drawn away, away...

As Yates and the Doctor started down the cellar steps to help her, Sarah Jane Smith flicked out of existence. By the time they reached the mandala it was empty...

6

Arrival on Metebelis Three

Sarah landed – somewhere – with a jolt, eyes tight shut.
At first she didn't dare open them, for fear of what she
might see. But she couldn't prevent the impressions of
her surroundings flooding in. It was hot. Dry and hot.
Yet at the same time the air had a sort of richness, a
not-unpleasant spicy tang, as if it contained elements
she wasn't used to. Underfoot, she could feel sand and
pebbles . . .

She opened her eyes, and saw yellow sandstone. She
was sheltering under a huge boulder. Other boulders,
fantastically shaped, were dotted about a tawny, desert-
like landscape. A range of blue mountains towered in
the distance. Most astonishing of all, the desert was
strewn with a carpet of many-coloured, shining gem-
stones. Instinctively, Sarah knew where she was. Somehow she had been swept up in the power of Lupton's
ritual. She was on Metebelis Three.

A flicker of movement caught her eye. A solitary figure
was plodding across that jewelled plain, towards the high-
est mountain. Even at this distance, Sarah could recognise Lupton. She decided that wherever *he* was going,
she didn't want to, and turned firmly in the other direction. Not far away was a patch of green, cultivated
fields edging a sparkling river, and, near that, a settlement of little huts. 'I hope the natives are friendly,'
thought Sarah.

As she left the shelter of her boulder, someone pounced
from behind. A grimy, work-hardened hand clamped

down over her mouth; a sinewy, bare arm locked across her throat. Some kind of cloak was thrown over her head, and despite her frantic struggle, she was picked up and carried off.

During a hot, bumpy and very uncomfortable journey, Sarah could only discover that her unseen captor was thin and wiry – but very strong. He quelled with ease her attempts to struggle, and carried her what seemed a very long way with no sign of tiredness.

At last she was dumped down abruptly, on a very hard surface. The cloak was whipped from her head, and she blinked in the sudden light. She was in a roughly cobbled village square, surrounded by one-storey log buildings.

Around her stood a little group of people in rough working clothes. They looked like Middle Ages peasants, with a few exotic touches. An argument was raging over her head.

'I tell you she's a spy,' someone was saying. 'I found her hiding in the rocks.' He was a tall, fierce-looking youth – obviously the one who had captured her.

One of the women said angrily, 'Then why bring her here and endanger us all, Tuar? You should have killed her where you found her.'

Tuar nodded. 'You're right. But it's easily remedied.' He pulled out a knife and started towards Sarah.

She screamed, scrambled to her feet, and tried to run – but she was hemmed in. 'I'm *not* a spy,' she babbled. 'I don't know who you are or anything about you.'

'You lie,' said Tuar, reaching out for her again.

Sarah backed away. 'Who am I supposed to be spying for – the spiders?'

A gasp of horror issued from the little group. 'You see,' said Tuar, 'she *is* a spy. Who but one of the eight-legs' creatures would dare use the forbidden word?'

Hands grabbed Sarah and held her helpless, as Tuar approached with his knife. A voice said 'Stop!' A tall handsome man in his thirties had come out of one of the houses, and was striding towards them. Sarah could see by the way people fell back before him that he was some kind of leader. 'Don't harm her, Tuar,' he ordered. 'I think she's telling the truth. Look at her clothes – she's a stranger. A spy would try to pass for one of us, or someone from the next village. She doesn't even look as if she came from this planet.'

'I don't!' said Sarah eagerly. 'I come here from Earth.'

The man looked at her keenly. 'How? In a starship like our ancestors?' A sudden hope showed in his face. 'Do you bring help from Earth against our oppressors?'

'I wish I did,' said Sarah. 'I came here alone – and I'm not even sure how I got here.'

Tuar, who seemed to be a young man of very fixed views, said, 'I tell you, brother, she's a spy! She will betray us all.'

A long, high trumpet note rang through the square. The effect on the little crowd was extraordinary. Everyone broke and ran for the shelter of the huts. From having been the centre of attention, Sarah suddenly found herself totally ignored. Only the tall man had not run with the others. He looked at her consideringly for a moment and said, 'You'd better come with me. We'll talk later.' He took Sarah by the wrist and pulled her across the square and into one of the huts, shutting the door behind them.

There were a number of people already crowded into the little hut, including Tuar, and an older man and woman, both with lined, toil-worn faces. Sarah's rescuer waved his hand around the hut. 'Welcome,' he said. 'This is my brother, Tuar, whom you have already met. These are my parents, Sabor and Neska.'

It seemed odd to be exchanging introductions with people who, seconds ago, had been planning to kill her, but Sarah did her best. 'How do you do,' she said politely. 'My name is Sarah.' Tuar just glared at her. The old people looked at her with frightened faces. The trumpet sounded again, very near this time. Everyone crowded to the window. Sarah joined them, trying to see what was going on.

Four men marched into the square. Two carried a richly decorated conveyance rather like a small sedan chair. On the chair rested a cushion, and on the cushion sat a giant spider, far larger than the one Sarah had seen at the monastery. Although Sarah didn't know it, this was the Queen Spider, who had talked with Lupton not long ago.

The men carrying the chair set it down. Then, with their two fellows, they formed a guard, one at each corner. They wore simple peasant-type clothes like the villagers, but their steel and leather trappings showed they were soldiers. All four carried short, jewelled staves. One of them, evidently their Captain, raised his jewelled staff and spoke in a kind of formal chant. 'Hear now! Huath, Queen of the eight-legs, most noble of the Noble Ones, speaks thus: Arak, male two-leg, having most wickedly attacked Field-Guard Draga, leaving him for dead, the same Arak will now surrender himself.'

Sarah listened to this rigmarole with astonishment. Then she realised with a shock that Arak, the man being called upon to surrender himself, was her rescuer.

Arak gave a sigh of resignation, and started to leave the hut. The old woman clung to him, and Tuar, his brother, barred his way. 'Don't go, brother. They'll kill you.'

Arak looked at him grimly. 'Listen to the rest of it.'

The hoarse voice of the guard carried clearly through the open window. 'If Arak does not surrender, one male two-leg will be taken from each family of the settlement to suffer the retribution due as a result of the foul crime of Arak.'

Gently, Arak disengaged Neska's arm. 'I must go, Mother, or we shall all suffer.'

Sabor, the old man, said quickly, 'Let me speak with the Queen. She may listen to me.'

'No,' snapped Arak. 'Why should you run the risk?'

'Because our people need you, my son,' said the old

man gently. 'They trust you and listen to you. You are our only hope.' Before anyone could stop him, the old man had slipped out of the door.

Through the window Sarah saw him run to the Spider's chair and kneel before it.

'I beg leave to speak to the Queen,' he called.

'Speak then, Sabor,' said the Queen. She spoke in the clear, cold voice of all the Spiders.

Sabor began to plead for his son, saying that Draga was a cruel guard who oppressed the villagers. The cold voice of the Queen cut through his words.

'He struck my guard, did he not? Then he must die. Where is he?'

Sabor stood up boldly. 'He has escaped to the hills. I helped him.'

'Then *you* will take his place,' said the Queen. 'Justice is satisfied. Let us return!'

The bearers lifted the chair, and the little procession moved off. Sabor walked between the two remaining guards, his head held high. Neska, his wife, broke free of her son's restraining hold and ran after him, sobbing and screaming. One of the guards touched her arm with his jewelled staff, and she collapsed, writhing in pain. People were appearing at the doors of the huts by now, but no one dared move to help her.

Sarah felt a sudden surge of blazing anger against the callousness of the Spider Queen. She glared angrily after the departing chair. Suddenly, the Queen's voice rang out again. 'Stop! I sense the presence of a stranger here. One who has the audacity not to fear me! Guards, search the village.'

Sarah turned to Arak. 'They mustn't find you here.' She turned and walked slowly out of the hut ...

After a hair-raisingly fast drive from the monastery in Bessie, the Doctor rushed into his laboratory, unlocked the TARDIS and disappeared inside. As his fingers flicked over the controls of the central console, he reflected grimly that, erratic as the TARDIS sometimes was, Metebelis Three was the one place he could be sure of reaching. Long ago, on his first trip in search of the blue crystal, he'd wired the co-ordinates into the programmer, and they'd never been removed. There was still the question of time, but he could safely leave that to the TARDIS – she had an instinct in these matters.

The Brigadier, hurrying into the laboratory to ask the Doctor how he'd got on, realised that he was too late. The familiar groaning noise filled the air and the old blue police box shimmered and disappeared . . .

For a direct linked journey like this in the TARDIS, departure and arrival were almost simultaneous. In no time at all, the Doctor was unlocking the TARDIS door and stepping out on to the soil of an alien planet.

He locked the TARDIS behind him, and then looked round, with a sudden feeling that he was not alone.

And indeed he was not. The TARDIS had landed in a sort of village square. The villagers were standing in the doorways of their huts, looking at him in awe. Directly in front of him stood a kind of sedan chair, on which sat a very large spider. And to complete the picture, Sarah was being held prisoner between two menacing guards. Sarah looked towards him in astonishment. 'Oh, Doctor,' she said, 'of all the times to arrive!'

7

Prisoner of the Spiders

The Doctor gave Sarah an encouraging smile, and said cheerfully, 'Hullo, Sarah Jane!' He walked straight towards the sedan chair on which sat the Spider. One of the guards touched him on the arm with his jewelled staff. The Doctor felt a sudden sharp pang, like a moderate electric shock. He jumped back, and said reprovingly, 'Do be careful, old chap. That hurts!'

The guard was taken aback. 'Kneel to the most noble Queen,' he growled.

'By all means,' said the Doctor obligingly. He made a courtly bow, in an elaborate style he'd learned at the court of good Queen Bess, and fell on one knee. 'Greetings, O Queen. May I ask what you're going to do with this young lady? You see, she's a friend of mine, and . . . '

The Queen interrupted him, 'Where do you come from?'

'Both Sarah and I come from Earth.'

'Bring him too,' ordered the Queen Spider. 'He must be questioned.'

One of the guards tried to shove the Doctor towards Sarah and Sabor. When the Doctor didn't move, the guard jabbed him with the staff. This time the pain was sharper and the Doctor didn't care for it at all. 'I *did* ask you not to do that,' he said mildly, then picked the guard up and threw him across the square. The astonished man cartwheeled away in a whirl of arms and legs, and landed against one of the huts with a thump. Two more guards made for the Doctor, and he threw them after the first one, who was just getting up. All three went down again.

Suddenly Sarah yelled, 'Doctor, look out!' The Doctor whirled round to see the guard Captain raise his staff in a pointing gesture. The Doctor dodged, and the blast of energy whizzed past him. By now the guards were on him again and there followed a short, confused struggle, which the Doctor enjoyed enormously. So, too, did the people of the village, who crowded to their doorsteps to enjoy the spectacle of the Spider Queen's guards being knocked about like skittles! When it was over, only the Doctor was still on his feet.

He was reaching out a hand to Sarah, when again she screamed, 'Doctor!' But this time the warning came too late. The Queen Spider was quivering with rage on her cushion. A crackling finger of flame lanced from her body and caught the Doctor squarely in the back. The force of it blasted him clean across the square and on to the TARDIS. He crashed against its door then slid down it, apparently dead. The Queen's voice rang out across the square: 'So perish all who dare to question our power.'

The villagers muttered angrily at the defeat of their champion. They began to press closer round the sedan, and the guards had a hard time holding them back. In the jostling of the crowd Sarah was pushed away from her guard, whose attention was taken up with the angry villagers. She felt a hand tugging at her own. A rough shawl was thrown over her head. Sarah drew it down to cover her head and shoulders. A crowd of village women pressed round her.

The guard Captain looked at the unruly mob. He whispered to the Queen, 'It would be wise to leave now.'

One of the struggling guards called, 'The girl – she's gone.'

The Captain looked round, but Sarah was lost in the milling crowd of beshawled village women.

'You will be punished,' said the Queen. 'But we cannot wait. Soon it will be dark. Bring the male!' Two guards picked up the chair; two others hustled Sabor away between them. The little procession left the square, and headed across the plain of jewels to the blue mountain.

As soon as they were out of sight, Sarah ran to the crumpled figure of the Doctor. He was white and still, no sign of life or movement about him.

Arak came to her side and tried to lead her away. 'It's no good. He's dead. They can use their powers to give pain or to stun, but the full blast kills. Your friend is *dead*.'

Sarah was on her knees beside the Doctor trying to find some kind of pulse. 'He isn't dead. He can't be.'

Tuar joined them. 'If we stay out here, we shall all be dead. It's almost curfew time.'

Sarah saw the rest of the villagers hurrying into their huts. She noticed for the first time that it was growing dark. 'Tuar's right,' said Arak gently. 'Leave him there. We'll bury him tomorrow.'

The two men began to pull her away from the Doctor by main force. At first Sarah was too desolate to resist them, then she began to struggle wildly. She tore herself free from their grip. 'Look! He moved. He moved his arm!' She ran back to the Doctor, the two men following. Suddenly the Doctor stirred and groaned. 'She's right,' said Arak incredulously. 'He *is* alive. Come on, give me a hand.' Lifting the Doctor between them, Arak and Tuar dragged him into their hut, Sarah following anxiously behind.

They stretched the Doctor out on a rough wooden bunk. A young woman, the one who had given Sarah the shawl, came into the hut. Arak nodded towards her. 'This is Rega, my sister. How is Mother?'

'Sleeping. She moans and calls Sabor's name.'

The Doctor, too, was moaning and twisting on his bed. The woman looked down at him.

Sarah said worriedly. 'He seems to be getting worse.'

The woman nodded. 'He's dying, my child. No one can survive the anger of the eight-legs.'

The slow tolling of a bell resounded through the village, 'What's that?' asked Sarah.

Tuar looked out of the window. 'Curfew! It's death to be out after twilight. The patrols kill on sight.'

The Doctor groaned again. 'Is there nothing you can do?' pleaded Sarah.

Rega looked at her with the calmness of one well used to death and suffering. 'Nothing. By rights he should be dead already.'

Another visitor to Metebelis Three was in somewhat better condition. Lupton, following the instructions of his Spider, had plodded across the jewelled plain until he reached the base of the blue mountain. He had come to a little group of scattered huts which encircled a pool. There, guards had appeared and handled him roughly until his Spider had materialised and frightened them into instant submission. The Spider scuttled away into the mountain. The guards treated Lupton with reverence, taking him into one of the little huts and giving him refreshment. Lupton had drunk fiery blue wine, and eaten chunks of roasted mutton, rough, whole-ground bread, and strange exotic fruits. Then they had led him through the network of caves into the heart of the mountain. The tunnels were lit by flickering torches, and blue jewels glinted in their walls. At last he stood in the shadowy place that he had visited once before in his mind: the Council Chamber of the Spiders.

Lupton's Spider was playing for time, giving a long account of her adventures on Earth. Lupton listened keenly, well aware that his own fate depended on her winning the Council's trust. But the Queen, freshly returned from her experiences in the village, was in an evil mood. She threatened the Spider with the anger of the 'Great One', who seemed to be some kind of supreme ruler, and even more powerful than the Queen. Lupton gathered that she lived a solitary existence somewhere in the depths of the blue mountains, although her influence was felt everywhere. 'You waste our time,' said the Queen finally. 'Where *is* the crystal?'

Paralysed with fear, the Spider made no answer. Lupton decided to intervene. He knew that if his Spider revealed that they had *lost* the crystal, they would both be killed instantly. If they were going to bluff, they might as well be bold about it. '*We* have the crystal, O Queen,' said Lupton, with a confidence he was far from feeling.

'Then where *is* it? The Council waits for it. So too does the Great One!'

'Then the Council will continue to wait – until we have received the rewards of our success!'

A murmur of horror ran through the Council. 'Such insolence, from a mere two-legs,' they muttered.

'Guards, seize him,' snapped the Queen. The guards lining the edge of the Chamber rushed forward.

'You dare not harm us,' said Lupton. 'Remember *we* have the crystal.'

'Stop,' called the Queen. The guards fell back. The Queen's mind raced furiously. She would *not* be humiliated in her own Council Chamber. Suddenly she remembered the events at the village and her agile mind saw how to turn them to her advantage.

'It appears that you do not realise the extent of your *failure*. You were followed here by two Earth spies. The male I killed. The other, a girl, still lives. I suggest, sisters, that we refuse to listen to these traitors, until she is captured. Then it will be time to discuss rewards.'

A fierce hum of assent went up from the Council. The guards began once more to close in on Lupton. He decided to try a final piece of boldness.

'Then permit me to help you, O Queen. I know the girl you speak of. I met her on Earth.' He gestured to the guards around him. 'Give me the assistance of these gentlemen, and I'll capture her for you myself.'

Sarah crouched over the sleeping Doctor, alert for every flicker of his eyelids. From time to time, she sponged his brow with fresh water from a stone jug. Behind her, Arak and his brother were arguing fiercely. Sarah was dimly aware that the younger and more hot-headed Tuar was urging open revolt, while Arak insisted that this would be mere suicide. They must wait for some better opportunity – though what opportunity he could not say. They needed help.

'No one can help us,' said Tuar fiercely. 'We must save ourselves.'

Sarah looked up. 'The Doctor could help you, if he was well again. I'm sure he could.'

As if in response to his name, the Doctor stirred. 'Sarah,' he muttered, 'Sarah?'

She leaned closer to him. 'I'm here, Doctor.' His eyes flickered open and fixed on hers. He seemed to be struggling to tell her something of immense importance. 'Machine!' he said indistinctly. 'Need machine – cure me.'

'What machine, Doctor? Tell me where it is.'

'Machine in TARDIS – in old leather bag . . . left hand locker . . .' The Doctor's voice tailed away, and his head fell back. Sarah found the TARDIS key on its thong round his neck and gently lifted it over his head.

'Machine?' said Arak. 'Why does he want a machine?'

Sarah was on her feet. 'I don't know, but if he needs it, I'm going to get it.' She headed for the door but Arak stopped her.

'You *can't* go out. They'll catch and kill you.'

'I'll have to risk that.' She slipped past him, out of the hut.

The cobbled square was still and silent in the blue moonlight. Sarah slipped off her shoes, leaving them at the hut door. Her bare feet made no sound on the cobbles. The TARDIS sat incongruously in the middle of the square. Sarah reached it in one quick, silent dash. She opened the door and slipped inside.

Hurriedly she went to the Doctor's locker. It was his odds-and-ends locker, and held the most amazing assortment of junk from every planet and time. At last she found what she was looking for: a beautifully decorated leather bag, with a machine inside. Sarah took a quick look at it. It was a complicated arrangement of coiled metal, with something that looked like a hand-grip. Sarah shut the bag and left the TARDIS. The heavy bag was cumbersome, and she dropped it at her feet while she locked the TARDIS door.

She was about to sprint back to the hut, when someone stepped from behind the TARDIS and barred her way. It was Lupton. He sneered in the manner that she remembered from their first meeting in the monastery. 'You *are* keen to get a story, aren't you, Miss Smith? What a pity it'll never be published.'

Sarah dodged round him, and ran across the square. A guard stepped out from the shadows. She turned. More guards were coming towards her. Sarah dodged and weaved away from them. She knew there was no chance of escape. Her one aim was to lead the guards as far away from the TARDIS, and Arak's cottage, as she possibly could.

She had reached the far end of the village when they finally caught her. She collapsed, gasping from lack of breath, and they soon had her held fast. Lupton came up, smiling with satisfaction. He snapped his fingers, and the guards dragged Sarah away. The leather bag, with the Doctor's machine inside, lay forgotten in a pool of shadow at the foot of the TARDIS. Forgotten, that is, by Lupton, and the guards, who had scarcely ever been aware of it. But not forgotten by Arak, who had watched the whole scene from the doorway of his hut. 'She led them away from us,' he said softly. 'And the bag is still there – at the foot of the stranger's machine.' He glanced at the Doctor who lay deathly still on his bunk. 'The girl said this man could help us. I'm going to get the machine.'

Before anyone could protest, Arak slipped out into the darkness of the square.

He was taking a calculated risk. The patrol that had captured Sarah would be busy taking her to the Spiders. The next patrol wasn't due for ten minutes or more.

Like Sarah before him, Arack sprinted across the square on bare, silent feet, and dropped panting into the shadows at the foot of the TARDIS. The bag was still there. He picked it up, amazed at the weight, paused to recover his breath and prepared to set off back to his hut. Then he heard the ringing of booted feet on the cobblestones. The second patrol had come early!

He could see them approach as he peered round the edge of the TARDIS: big, cruel-looking men, carrying blazing torches to search out anyone hiding in the shadows, armed with the jewelled staffs that all the Spiders' servants carried – weapons that could paralyse or kill. Arak knew they would patrol the whole square. They would see him if he waited; they would see him if he moved.

Arak's bare toe stubbed against one of the cobbles. It was loose! Scrabbling desperately, he worked it free. He crouched, hefting it in his hand, a round stone about the size of an apple . . . Arak hurled the stone high across the roof of a nearby house. It landed in the alley behind, with a clatter that *might* have been made by an escaping fugitive. Instantly the patrol was alerted. Raising their torches they ran down the alleyway in pursuit. The bag under his arm, Arak dashed back to his hut. Tuar was holding the door open. Arak shot inside, and Tuar closed the door silently behind him.

Arak took the odd-looking machine from the bag. 'Well, there it is. Though what we're supposed to do with it . . . '

'Maybe *he'll* know,' said Tuar, jerking his head towards the Doctor.

They laid the machine on the Doctor's chest. He reacted quickly, gripping it convulsively. At once the

74

machine seemed to come to life. It started emitting a low powerful hum. Lights glowed and flashed somewhere inside it. Arak, Tuar and Rega looked on in amazement. Suddenly a powerful spark raced out of the Doctor's body, through the machine, and into the ground. It was as though the evil energy was being drained from the Doctor's body. He stiffened, then relaxed limply. He opened his eyes suddenly and said distinctly, 'Thank you. Thank you very much.' He closed them, and went peacefully to sleep.

* * * * *

The guards marched Sarah deeper and deeper into the complex of caverns that was the home of the Spiders. They led her down a long gloomy tunnel, and then into a small, round chamber. Strands of cobwebby stuff festooned the walls and ceilings. A long cocoon of the same stuff hung from one wall. To her horror, Sarah saw projecting from one end the head of the old man Sabor, Arak's father.

Holding her firmly, the guards stripped some of the white sticky stuff from the walls and began to wrap it round her. Panic-stricken, she started to struggle – but it was too late. The sticky web held her fast. She could barely move. They cocooned her from neck to feet, leaving her, like Sabor, with only her head projecting. Then they carried her across the chamber and propped her up beside him. The cocoon stuck fast to the walls. She was helpless.

Lupton had been looking, a familiar sneer on his face. When the process was complete, he said, 'Do you know where you are, Miss Smith?'

'Why should I?' snapped Sarah defiantly. 'I assume it's some kind of a prison?'

'How little you know of the habits of our eight-legged friends, Miss Smith,' said Lupton with evident relish. 'You're not in a prison. You're in the larder.'

8

The Doctor Hits Back

Dawn was approaching on Metebelis Three. The planet's huge, bright sun, far closer to Metebelis than our sun is to Earth, was rising rapidly. The gem-stones of the desert reflected its rays in a hundred different colours. In the village, the humans stirred uneasily, knowing that it would soon be time to go and toil in the fields for their Spider rulers.

In Arak's hut threee men still slept: the Doctor on the bunk, Arak and Tuar sprawled on the floor. The Doctor woke first. A ray of sunshine came through the window and touched his face. He snapped instantly awake, like a human alarm clock. He felt rested, and fighting fit. He looked at his two sleeping companions and his eyes began to twinkle mischievously. He flung back the rough curtains, and sunlight flooded into the little hut. The two brothers stirred and muttered. The Doctor said loudly, 'Wakey, wakey, rise and shine, show a leg the morning's fine!' Arak and Tuar blinked, and muttered. They turned their heads towards the Doctor in astonishment, wondering how a man who had been good as dead the night before could wake up so appallingly cheerful! The Doctor looked at them hopefully. 'How about a spot of breakfast?'

Soon the Doctor was tucking into a plate of thick broth, brought to him by Rega. Cold water and hard bread made up the rest of the meal, but the Doctor ate with the greatest enjoyment. 'Excellent broth, this,' he said. 'What is it?'

Tuar grunted, 'Mutton . . .' He went on eating.

'You have sheep on Metebelis?' said the Doctor chattily. He held out his bowl for more broth. Rega poured it from a stone jug.

Arak said patiently, 'Our ancestors brought them from Earth.'

'Colonists?'

Arak nodded. 'Four hundred and thirty-three years ago, a starship came out of its time jump with no power left and crashed on Metebelis Three.' He spoke in a sort of formal chant.

The Doctor looked at him curiously. 'You seem to know the story very well.'

'My father taught it to me – and his to him.'

'A detailed oral tradition. Fascinating! And what about the spiders?'

Arak was surprised. 'I thought you knew – they came from Earth too. We think there must have been a colony of them somewhere on the ship. When it crashed, they were blown free. The wind carried them to the blue mountain.'

'Yes of course,' said the Doctor. It was all falling into place now.

'The Earth Spiders went to live in the blue mountains,' said Arak. 'The crystals enlarged the spiders' bodies and minds.'

Tuar took up the story. 'Over the years the eight-legs grew larger and larger, cleverer and cleverer. Their minds acquired the power to control humans – to blast us down with pure thought. Eventually they took over.'

'How did they manage to do that – and how do they *stay* in charge?'

'With the help of traitors,' said Arak bitterly. 'When they saw how things were going, some humans joined the eight-legs. Now they help to enslave the rest of us. *They* don't work in the fields. They get the pick of the crops, while we nearly starve. The Spiders even share a few of their powers with them – just to keep the rest of us in line.'

'Like those jewelled staves,' said the Doctor. 'They

must act as telepathic amplifiers.' Though the technique *could* work without them, he thought. Lupton hadn't needed one – or the Queen Spider.

Tuar suddenly exploded. 'I don't understand you,' he shouted. 'Our father is a prisoner of the eight-legs! So is that girl, your friend. Yet you sit there supping broth, and discussing ancient history. The girl said you would *help* us!'

'And so I will,' said the Doctor. 'But first I had to know exactly what I was up against.' He went over to the back window and looked out. Behind the hut, the jewelled desert stretched away to the distant blue mountains. 'I want you to bring me some gems,' he said suddenly. 'Like those lying out there on the plain. As many as you can, all different shapes, sizes and colours.'

'Those gems are useless,' protested Tuar. 'They're everywhere. We even have to clear them from our fields when we plough. There's a pile of them behind the village.'

Arak nodded. 'The blue crystals of power are found only on the mountains. They're scarce now – the eight-legs hunt for them constantly.'

'There's more than one kind of crystal on Metebelis,' said the Doctor, 'and more than one kind of power. You get me those stones, and I'll get you a weapon against the Spiders.'

Tuar looked at his brother. Arak shrugged. 'We have nothing to lose. Take a sack and go to the stone pile.'

Sulkily Tuar obeyed.

Ten minutes later the floor of the little hut was covered with stones. The Doctor sat in the middle of them, his machine in his lap. The machine was switched on again, and humming quietly. The Doctor picked up a stone and held it to the machine. There was a low electronic buzz, and he tossed the stone to one side. He tested another, and another, still with the same result. Arak and Tuar looked on, the latter with mounting impatience, as the Doctor worked patiently. Finally Tuar could restrain himself no longer. 'My father and your friend are in peril and you play these childish games . . .'

The Doctor held up a hand to silence him. 'Sssh! I think I've got it!' The last stone he had tested had produced an altogether different reaction from the machine – a high, clearer buzz. He tested the stone again. 'Excellent!' said the Doctor. 'Now we can get a move on.' He put the machine on the bed and said, 'Both of you, help me sort through these stones. All we're interested in are stones exactly like this.' The Doctor held out his hand. On his palm lay an undistinguished-looking piece of brown quartz, flecked with green. Tuar looked as if he would explode again, but Arak forestalled him.

'It would help if you told us why, Doctor,' he said.

The Doctor looked at him in mild astonishment. 'Oh, didn't I explain?' Even as he spoke, the Doctor was sifting though the pile of coloured gem-stones for more pieces of quartz. 'The *blue* crystals magnify the power of the mind. Now, since most things have their opposites, I was looking for a stone which deadened it. Something to soak up the energy of the Spiders' mental attacks. Luckily for all of us, I think I've found one. So if you'd kindly give me some help . . .'

Hurriedly, Arak and Tuar joined in the hunt. As usual, the Doctor had taken charge.

By the time the morning was well advanced, an amazing amount had been done. The quartz was extremely common, and hundreds of the little brown stones had been found.

Runners from Arak's resistance organisation were carrying specimen stones, and the Doctor's instructions, to all the other villages. Meanwhile, Rega and the other village women, following more instructions from the Doctor, were making simple rag headbands, each with one of the little brown stones sewn into the front. Rega brought the first batch to the Doctor for his approval. 'Is this what you wanted?'

The Doctor picked up the strip of linen with its little

79

stone. 'Excellent. Come here, Arak, old chap.' The Doctor stood behind Arak and tied the band round his head. He adjusted it carefully, so that the stone rested exactly in the centre of Arak's forehead. 'There we are – splendid!'

Arak raised his hand and touched the headband dubiously. '*This* will protect me from the eight-legs – and from the jewelled staves of their guards?'

The Doctor nodded.

Tuar rushed into the hut, and looked curiously at his brother's new headdress. 'There's a patrol heading for the village,' he gasped.

Arak turned to the Doctor. 'A chance to test your "protection", Doctor. If it doesn't work, they'll wipe this village out.'

The squad of guards, jewelled staves in their hands, swung confidently into the village, as they had done many times before. They halted with a crash of booted feet in the centre of the square. The Captain gazed around him. The men of the village were gathering in front of their huts. 'Why do you not work in the fields?' he shouted. 'Go at once! You will all be punished.' There was no reply. A tall man detached himself from the gathering crowd and walked steadily towards the guards. He wore a strange sort of headband. The Captain saw that the other men were wearing them too. He looked again at the tall man, and his eyes widened. 'It is the traitor, Arak!' he shouted. 'He is to be killed on sight!'

The tall man came steadily on. The Captain raised his jewelled staff, summoned the power of his mind, and channelled a blast of energy *through* the staff and on to the approaching rebel. He waited to see the man collapse in agony. Nothing happened. Arak still came marching towards him. The stern, cold face under the incongruous headband was the last thing the Captain saw. Arak's big hands reached for his throat, and everything went black . . .

The rest of the guards panicked and turned to run. But there were men everywhere, men with strips of cloth bound round their heads. It was all over in a matter of minutes. Arak stood at the doorway of his hut and called out, 'Hide the bodies. We must keep everything looking normal as long as possible. If they send others, deal with them in the same way. Not a guard must get back to warn the eight-legs!' He turned to the Doctor who stood beside him ready to depart. 'I'm sorry, Doctor. It's necessary.'

The Doctor nodded sadly. He knew there was no gentle way of breaking the grip of the terror that had held Metebelis for so long. But, as always, the taking of life saddened and sickened him. 'I must go now, Arak,' he said. 'Follow me as soon as you can.'

'Doctor – you have no stone to protect you.'

The Doctor tapped the leather bag on his shoulder. 'Don't worry. I have something better.' The two men clasped hands, and the Doctor left the village and set off across the jewelled desert to the blue mountain.

He was going to confront the Spiders in their web.

Evening was approaching by the time he arrived at the end of his long and lonely journey. He saw the guard settlement in the foothills that Lupton had found, and avoided it. Arak had told him there were other, less well-guarded entrances to the mountain – and he was right. After an hour's scrambling about the foothills, he found a narrow cave which was partially concealed by a boulder. It was the entrance to a tunnel that stretched deep down into the mountain. Cautiously, the Doctor began to move along it.

In the heart of the mountain itself, Sarah twisted restlessly in her cocoon. She had long lost count of the time she had spent in the Spiders' larder, but it seemed ages and ages! 'Maybe they're well stocked up,' she thought hopefully. Every now and again she had a burst of frantic struggling, but her sticky clinging bonds were immovable. Old Sabor looked on sadly. 'It is no use, my child. Even your young muscles are not strong enough. Try to rest.'

'Rest? How can you be so calm?'

'One is only frightened when there is still hope. We have none.'

Not the most inspiring of companions, thought Sarah to herself. After a moment she said, 'Was Lupton – the other man from Earth – telling the truth? Will they really – eat us?'

Sabor nodded. 'Usually they eat the sheep we breed for them. Otherwise they would be devouring their own servants. But they prefer human flesh – when they have an excuse.'

Sarah shuddered. She renewed her struggles. 'We've *got* to get away.'

Sabor hung passively in his cocoon.

'I tell you there is no hope.'

'There's *always* hope,' said Sarah fiercely. 'Maybe the Doctor will come and rescue us.'

'Accept it, my child,' said Sabor. 'We are already dead.'

The Doctor followed the tunnel even deeper into the mountain. It was partially blocked with rubble that he had to climb over, and around. He guessed that it was more or less disused. Then the tunnel ran into another one, broader and lit with flaring torches. The Doctor could see blue crystals, which were inset in the walls. He had reached the heart of the mountain, where the Spiders lived – and their guards. From now on his journey would be ever more dangerous, but he had to go on. The Doctor took the machine from its leather bag and prepared it for use. He moved out cautiously into the main tunnel.

For a while his luck held. But as he turned a corner, he ran straight into a guard. Automatically, the guard raised his jewelled staff – and the Doctor raised his machine. It was a considerably more sophisticated piece of work than the improvised headbands, and its effects went one stage further. Not only did it absorb the effect of the mental energy-blast and render it harmless – it stored the power and flung it back upon the attacker. Struck down by the force of his own attack, the guard screamed and crumpled to the floor. Unfortunately for the Doctor, there were other guards near by, and the sound of their companion's scream brought them running. The Doctor raised his machine to repel their attack, but yet another guard jumped him from behind, knocking the machine from his hands.

The Doctor disposed of this new opponent with a swift throw, but by now the guards were upon him. The machine had been knocked a few feet along the tunnel. If he could get to it before they reached him . . . He made a desperate leap forward, his body parallel with the ground.

The machine was inches from his fingers, when a foot stamped down upon his wrist. The foot was wearing an old and scruffy brown shoe. The Doctor looked up. Standing over him was Lupton.

The Doctor wrenched his wrist free. But before he could take the machine, Lupton's other foot booted it out of reach. The Doctor got up slowly. Surrounding him were at least six guards. Each one held a jewelled staff; each staff was pointing at the Doctor.

Lupton stepped back, licking his lips. 'Well, what are you waiting for? Kill him!'

9

In the Lair of the Great One

The Doctor braced himself. He knew even his extraordinary physique would be unable to survive the crystal-magnified impact of six hate-filled minds.

Another guard, a Captain, came running up, 'Stop!' The guards lowered their staves.

Lupton was furious. 'Obey my orders. Kill him.'

'I come from the Queen,' said the Captain. 'Arrest *him* and take him to the Council.' He pointed at Lupton. Protesting furiously, Lupton was bundled away by two of the guards.

The Doctor shook his head sadly. 'Poor fellow. Hope they won't be to hard on him. Got into bad company, you know.' With a friendly nod, the Doctor started to stroll away.

For a moment, the Captain was so astonished at his audacity that he almost let the Doctor go. Then he made a sign to the remaining guards, who leaped on the Doctor and pinioned him. 'Your execution has merely been postponed,' said the Captain sourly, 'Take him away!'

Sarah's face filled with joy as the Doctor appeared in the doorway. Then it fell, as she saw the guards behind him 'Oh, Doctor, not again!'

Lupton and his Spider, meanwhile, were standing before the Council.

'Your conspiracy has been discovered,' the Spider Queen said gleefully. 'You will both die.'

'They know that we did not bring the crystal back to Metebelis,' whispered Lupton's Spider.

Lupton looked coolly at the Queen. 'How did you find out?'

'In the same way that we first traced it. We linked our minds in an attempt to discover where you had hidden it. We felt its vibrations through Time and Space. They were faint, distant. The crystal is still on Earth.'

'Do you know where?'

Reluctantly the Spider Queen said, 'We cannot pinpoint the location. We fear the crystal is under the protection of a mind that we cannot reach.'

'Then the position hasn't changed at all,' said Lupton triumphantly. 'If you plan to invade Earth, you still need my help.'

The Queen almost hissed with rage. 'Be careful, two-legs! You will go too far.'

Sensing the change of feeling in the Council, Lupton's Spider added her efforts to his. 'What he says is true, O Queen. Once more your arrogance has endangered the master plan of the Council – the invasion of Earth.'

The Queen was silent. Pressing her advantage, the Spider went on. 'This is not the first mistake the Queen has made. Maybe she is growing old. Maybe it is time for a Coronation.'

Since the main feature of a Spider Coronation is the ceremonial eating of the old Queen by her successor, the Spider Queen reacted violently to this suggestion. She sought desperately for some move that would restore her power.

Suddenly she produced her trump card. 'I am not sure as to the wisdom of this invasion plan. I shall visit the Cave of the Crystal and consult the Great One. *Her* orders were to recover the crystal – nothing more.'

A ritual chant went up from the Council. 'All praise to the Great One!'

Her sisters eyed the Queen with new respect. It was true that the Great One had not been formally consulted about the projected invasion of Earth – and she had grown unpredictable of late. If any of her servants dis-

85

pleased her, even in thought, a colossal blast of mental energy sent them shrieking into nothingness. And the Great One was easily displeased. Few dared to visit her, or even to mention her name, lest that vast, scheming mind should turn upon them. Even to approach her too closely meant death.

'Do you hear me, *sisters*?' shrieked the Queen triumphantly. 'I shall, this very day, speak with the Great One herself! She will decide.'

Helplessly cocooned, like Sabor and Sarah, the Doctor flexed his muscles experimentally. 'Fascinating experience this,' he said cheerfully. 'I've often wondered what a fly feels like.'

'Well now you know,' said Sarah. 'You realise we're probably on tomorrow's menu?'

'Well, they'll find me a tough old bird,' said the Doctor determinedly. 'Now listen to me, both of you. Arak is gathering an army from the other villages . . . He's going to attack and rescue us.'

Sabor was horrified. 'He mustn't. It's certain death.'

'No, not now. I've given them a way to protect themselves. You see, I . . .'

The Doctor fell silent as the guard Captain re-entered the chamber. Another guard was with him, carrying a strangely shaped saw-edged knife – rather like a butcher's knife. The Captain pointed. 'The girl.'

Sarah screamed as the guard came towards her, knife raised. With a sudden, practised movement he slit Sarah's cocoon from top to bottom. She fell out of it, and collapsed on the floor. Agonies of pins and needles shot through her body, as her long-constricted muscles refused to hold her. She fainted from the pain. The guard picked her up, slung her over his shoulder, and carried her away.

'Where are you taking her?' shouted the Doctor.

The Captain looked coldly at him. 'Your turn will come.' He turned and followed the guard. Frantically the Doctor began struggling to escape.

In Arak's village an army filled the square. Night was falling now, and the whole square blazed with torches. There was a low murmur of angry voices. Every man was armed, some with long-hidden knives and, swords, others with scythes, bill-hooks and pitchforks – anything with an edge would do to kill a Spider guard. Every man wore a cloth headband with a brown gem-stone sewn into it.

Arak raised his hand, and the murmuring was stilled. 'Remember – we have nothing to fear. The Doctor has given us protection. Are we all ready?' A savage roar went up in reply. Arak's voice rang out in a triumphant shout. 'Forward, then! Death to the Eight-legs!' Arak's mind formed the word that had been forbidden so long on Metebelis. The true name of the creatures that oppressed them. Exultantly, he shouted it out at the top of his voice. 'Death to the *Spiders*!'

The crowd took up the shout. 'Death to the Spiders!' Torches blazing, weapons gleaming, they left the village and set out across the jewelled plain. The women of the village stood silent, watching the line of torches moving across the darkness like a snake of fire. Then they returned to the loneliness of their huts – to wait.

*   *   *   *   *

The Doctor's cocoon was swinging violently to and fro with the force of his efforts to escape. Sabor watched him gloomily. 'I tell you it's impossible, Doctor . . .'

The Doctor spoke in short bursts, grunting with effort. 'Much as I admire your stoic acceptance . . . of the inevitable . . . Sabor old chap . . . I do wish you'd be quiet. What I'm trying to do . . . requires the utmost concentration.'

'What *are* you trying to do?'

'Little trick I learned from an old friend of mine . . . feller named . . . what was it . . . Hopkins . . . no . . . Heatherington . . . no, that wasn't it. Got it! Houdini. Harry Houdini!'

To his amazement, Sabor saw that the Doctor's head and shoulders were beginning to emerge from the mouth of the cocoon. Like a python changing its skin, the Doctor wriggled out, further and further, until at last he was free. He struggled out of the cocoon and got to his feet, stretching and trying to massage his muscles into some kind of life. He crossed to Sabor and tried to free him too, but the task was hopeless.

'It's no good, Sabor, I shall have to leave you. As soon as I can, I'll come back with one of those knives and set you free. Oh, and if you hear the sound of fighting, give a jolly good yell. Your son Arak and his merry men should be here soon.' With a cheery wave, the Doctor slipped out of the chamber.

In another part of the mountain, Sarah waited fearfully. She was in a small, richly decorated chamber. Physically, she was in better condition than she had been for some time. Silent women, obviously slaves of the Spiders, had massaged her cramped limbs back to life. They had brought her wine and fruit, and more important still, water and towels so that she could wash off the grime of imprisonment. Then they had disappeared silently, leaving her waiting. But waiting for what? Sarah hoped that it hadn't all been a Spider's version of fattening up food and dressing it for the table . . .

Suddenly, a huge Spider appeared in the doorway. She scuttled across the floor and leaped on to a jewelled cushion.

Sarah cowered away.

The Spider spoke, in her high clear voice. 'You have no reason to fear me. I am the Queen. I am going to help you.'

'Why should you want to help me?'

'I do not agree with the plans of the Council – whether the Great One supports them or not. To invade the planet Earth would be a foolhardy venture. Why should we risk all that we possess here on Metebelis?'

Sarah understood little of what the Queen Spider was

88

saying. She listened alertly, trying to see what all this had to do with herself and the Doctor.

'I told them I would consult the Great One. But I shall not!' The Queen went on, 'I have lied to the Council. I intend to help you and the Doctor to escape to Earth.'

'Why?' asked Sarah bluntly.

The Queen's reply was indirect. 'Do you know of the blue crystal?' Sarah nodded.

'Then where is it?'

'Lupton's got it. He stole it from the Doctor.'

'He does not have it now,' said the Spider bitterly. 'It is still on Earth.'

Suddenly Sarah understood. 'And you want me and the Doctor to get it for you?'

'Yes – you must bring it to *me*. Not to the Council, and not to the Great One. To *me*. Otherwise there will be war between our peoples, and disaster for us all.' The Spider twitched restlessly on her cushion. 'Already rebellion is beginning on this planet. Many patrols have disappeared. How can we invade another planet when we are in danger of losing our own?'

Sarah wondered what the Queen Spider would say if she knew that the Doctor was behind the rebellion – that even now an army was on its way? She decided she'd better accept the offer while there was still time. Once they were away from this horrible planet, and back on Earth, the Doctor would sort things out somehow.

'All right,' she said quickly. 'Get us back to Earth and we'll help you. What do we do now?'

'Concentrate your mind,' said the Queen Spider. 'I shall lend you some of my powers . . . Turn your back, my child . . .'

The Doctor moved swiftly through the tunnels, keeping in shadow as best he could. Several times he had to duck into dark corners to avoid patrols. Without the machine, taken from him when he was first captured, he would be helpless against the power of the jewelled staves. To avoid detection, he was forced to move further and further away from the busier areas. Soon he found himself in an unlit disused tunnel, like the one by which he had entered. The Doctor paused to consider his next move.

Arak and his army would be here soon. He'd stand a far better chance of rescuing Sarah with their help. He decided to lie low until the fighting started, and then join up with them. Suddenly he heard a voice calling from the depths of the tunnel that stretched away before him. 'Doctor, Doctor!' It was Sarah. He must have stumbled on her place of imprisonment! Scarcely believing his good luck, the Doctor began to follow the sound of the voice. Somehow it seemed to be always just ahead of him. There it was again. 'Help, Doctor, help!' The Doctor ran on, ever deeper into the blue mountain.

He noticed that the tunnel walls around him were taking on a different look. The blue crystals were scattered ever more thickly. Soon they began to give off a glow of blue light. More, even fiercer, blue light shone ahead of him. The Doctor paused, wondering where he was coming to. This part of the mountain was quite different from anything he had seen before.

Still Sarah's voice lured him on. 'Doctor, help me! Please help me!' The more he hesitated, the more anguished her cries became.

Suddenly the tunnel came to an end. It opened out into a huge blue cavern. The walls seemed to have been carved out of one enormous blue crystal of tremendous size. The Doctor shielded his eyes against the pulsing light. There, at the back of the cavern was a gigantic crystal web, stretching away into the darkness.

A blue haze seemed to hang in front of it, partly concealing it from his view.

'Do not come any further, Doctor. Otherwise you will die.' The voice was high pitched and edgy, like chalk squeaking on a slate.

The Doctor felt the sudden pressure of a mind so powerful that it threatened to swallow up his own. 'I came to find Sarah,' he said calmly. 'I heard her calling to me.'

A sinister chuckle ran through the cave. 'Like *this*, Doctor?' asked the voice coyly. To the Doctor's horror, Sarah's voice came from the centre of the web.

> 'Half a pound of tuppeny rice
> Half a pound of treacle
> That's the way the money goes . . .'

'Pop goes the weasel,' finished the Doctor ruefully, realising how easily he had been tricked. His voice hardened. 'Who are you? What do you want with me?'

'I am the Great One. I want to help you, Doctor.'

The Doctor peered through the blue haze. Was there a vast shape in that web? 'Why can't I see you properly?'

'You will, Doctor, you will. All in good time. When you bring me the crystal you stole from me.'

The Doctor took another step forward.

'Stay!' said the voice imperiously. 'I tell you no one – *no one* – save myself may enter the cave of crystal and live. No two-legs, no eight-legs, not even the Queen herself – for all her boasting.'

The Doctor retreated. He suspected that she was telling the truth : that here in this amazing cave the vibrations of the blue crystals were so concentrated that they destroyed both body and mind. Presumably the Great One had somehow managed to adapt to them, but at what fearful cost?

As he retreated, he heard the piercing voice echoing round the cave. 'Go, Doctor. You must hurry back and fetch me the crystal. I must have it. I must have it. I must have it.'

As the Doctor hurried away, one thought dominated his mind. Whatever powers, whatever towering intelligence the Great One had attained, the price had been too high.

The Great One was mad.

The battle of the blue mountain was short and bloody. The Spiders' guards, so long accustomed to ruling by fear, so long dependent on the power of their jewelled staves, had little experience of real hand-to-hand fighting, and little taste for it.

Arak and his men fell upon them savagely, killing all who resisted them. The little army flooded into the tunnels, meeting and despatching guard after guard. Arak at their head, they penetrated deeper and deeper into the Spiders' fortress. The gloomy tunnels rang with the clash of arms, and the shouts of angry men.

Wrapped helpless in his cocoon, old Sabor listened with growing hope as the sound of fighting came ever nearer. Remembering the Doctor's advice, he began to shout, yelling until his throat was hoarse. At last he heard a familiar voice in reply.

'Father, it is I, Arak. I come!' Moments later, Arak ran into the chamber, Tuar at his heels. Both wore the protective headbands, both carried bloody swords in their hands. They rushed to the cocoon and cut Sabor free. They had to hold him upright between them, for he was far too weak to stand. Sabor was weeping with joy. Arak hugged him fiercely. 'Come, Father, we have work to do. Let us get you out of this accursed place.'

Supporting the old man between them, they left the chamber. As they went along the tunnels, Sabor said suddenly, 'The Doctor – is he with you? They took the girl and then the Doctor escaped . . .'

'We'll find him, Father,' said Tuar. 'All Metebelis owes him a great debt. Come!' Gently they led the old man towards the daylight that he had thought never to see again.

Sarah ran full tilt through the tunnels towards the

sound of battle. Once or twice, terrified, fleeing guards passed her, but they paid her no attention, concerned only with escaping from Arak and his men. Inside her head, Sarah could hear the voice of the Queen Spider. 'This way, my child. This way. I can sense that the Doctor is near . . .'

And, sure enough, the Doctor suddenly came dashing out of one of the side tunnels almost knocking Sarah over. He gripped her shoulders, overjoyed. 'Sarah, you're safe! Where have you been?'

She didn't seem to hear him. Her face was white and strained – naturally enough after all she'd been through, thought the Doctor.

'Listen, Doctor, we're going to escape,' she said. 'Hold my hands.'

The Doctor wondered if her terrible experiences had affected her mind, but decided to humour her. 'Of course we are,' he said soothingly.

'Hold my hands, Doctor.' Her voice was fierce and urgent. Wonderingly, the Doctor obeyed. Sarah's hands gripped his own tightly. The Doctor felt the sudden characteristic snatching sensation of teleportation, and found himself, still clasping hands with Sarah, standing by the TARDIS in the square of Arak's village.

'Pop goes the Weasel,' said the Doctor, for no very good reason. He looked at Sarah curiously. 'However did you learn to do that?'

Sarah grinned, looking more like her old self. 'Nothing to it really – the Queen taught me. Come on – I'll explain on the way back.'

The Doctor approached the door of the TARDIS. He felt around his neck, and turned to Sarah in consternation. 'The key – it's gone!'

'It's all right,' said Sarah soothingly. 'I've got it.' She unlocked the TARDIS' door, and held it open for him.

Just before going in, the Doctor paused. 'We seem to have been away quite a while. I wonder what's been happening back on Earth.'

10

Return to Earth

When all the excitement surrounding the disappearance of Lupton and Sarah had died down, Mike Yates found himself suffering from a powerful feeling of anti-climax. There had been no news of the Doctor since his mad dash back to the TARDIS, and Yates couldn't summon up the courage to call the Brigadier and ask him for an explanation.

The night after the disappearance there had been one minor mystery to divert his mind. Unable to sleep, he'd gone down to the library to get a book, and disturbed some mysterious visitor.

He'd caught a glimpse of a bulky figure disappearing through the French windows and thought it might be Tommy. But it didn't seem likely. Yates had then chosen a book for himself and gone to bed.

It wasn't till the afternoon of the following day that he got the feeling that things were happening again. Lupton's old cronies – Barnes, Moss, Keaver, and Lands – started gathering for whispered conversations in corners. Yates decided to keep an eye on them. It would give him something to do.

Meanwhile, in his cubby hole under the stairs, Tommy sat grappling with a tremendous problem. Something wonderful and frightening was happening to Tommy. He was starting to think. The transformation had begun just after Lupton, the Doctor, and Tommy's new friend Sarah, had all disappeared.

Tommy had tried to give Sarah the blue crystal for a present before she vanished. Now she had gone, he was left with it on his hands – and on his conscience. Tommy knew that it was wrong of him to have stolen the crystal from Lupton's room. His attempt to give it to Sarah had been a childish effort to transfer the burden of guilt. He couldn't even return it to Lupton, since Lupton had gone away too.

Tommy spent the rest of the day crouched in his tiny cupboard, studying the blue crystal and wondering what to do with it. The little glowing fires in the crystal seemed to soothe him. Then they seemed almost to talk to him, telling him that there were things he had to do. But what things?

He rummaged in his box of treasures and produced a tatty child's primer – a relic of the days before people had given up trying to teach him anything. He'd hung on to it in the vain hope that one day the mysterious black squiggles called letters would unlock their secrets. Now, with the blue crystal shining beside him, he tried again. Slowly at first, then quicker and quicker, he began to read. 'We go to school, we read our books, we play with our toys.' He raced through the little book in minutes, then buried his head in his hands, overcome by the wonder of it. He could read!

That night Tommy had sneaked down to the library and tried to read the books on the shelves. He stood enraptured by the poetry of William Blake.

Tyger, tyger, burning bright
In the forests of the night . . .

It was pretty. No, it was beautiful. Then, frightened by the arrival of Yates, he had fled. Perhaps he had been wrong to run. Yates was his friend. Yates had always been kind to him. Maybe he should go and look for him.

Yates, by now, was busy on his investigation. Pretending to sleep in the library, he'd seen Barnes chatting to Moss and Keaver, two of Lupton's old cronies. He could have sworn he heard the word 'meeting'. Still pretending to doze, he'd seen them all move off, making an elaborate pretence of going in different directions. Waiting enough time to give them a chance to get going, Yates rose to his feet and moved off after them.

His sandalled feet made no sound as he crept along the corridor. Barnes was the nearest thing to a leader, now that Lupton was gone. The meeting, if there was one, would be in his room. Yates moved quietly up to the door. Sure enough, a DO NOT DISTURB notice hung on the door-knob. Yates grinned. Talk about advertising! They were the most inept bunch of conspirators he'd ever had to tackle.

He bent down and put his ear to the keyhole. He could hear a low mumble of voices. He managed to pick out Barnes' voice. 'Lupton may not be dead. Maybe he just can't get back. If that's the case, we've got to try and help him. We must re-establish the link.'

Yates straightened up and smiled. It looked as if the conspirators' interests and his own were the same. He rapped firmly on the door.

There was a sudden tremendous flurry and scurry from inside. Yates rapped again and said, 'You might as well open up, Barnes. I'm coming in.'

One click and the door was unlocked. Barnes' voice called shakily, 'Come in then if you must.'

Yates went into the room. It was in semi-darkness, curtains drawn. A little reading lamp formed a pool of light around the armchair where Barnes sat, looking elaborately unconcerned. 'You may as well stop all this nonsense,' said Yates. 'Tell your friends to come out of hiding. I've been listening at the door and . . .' Lights exploded inside his skull, and everything went black.

Some time later, Yates woke up, gagged, bound hand and foot, with a nasty lump on the back of his head. He was on Barnes' bed. The room was empty. 'Fine investigator I made,' he thought to himself. It had never struck him that such a clownish bunch of plotters could be dangerous. He guessed that one of them had struck him

96

down in blind panic. Now they'd got him, they probably had no idea what to do next.

His theory was confirmed when Barnes came in and stood looking worriedly down at him. Yates made gurgling noises through his gag, indicating that he wanted to talk. After a moment Barnes hesitantly removed the gag. 'Well?' he said, with nervous truculence.

Yates licked his dry lips. 'What are you going to do – about Lupton?'

'What *can* we do?'

'I heard you talking, remember. You said you wanted to re-establish the link.'

Barnes glared at him suspiciously. 'What if I did?'

'It's just that I think you're quite right,' said Yates persuasively. 'Lupton's probably stranded somewhere, waiting for you to do just that. You can't *abandon* him.'

'The ritual really needs five of us. Lupton was the only one powerful enough to use it alone – now he's gone,' replied Barnes.

'I'll help you. That's what I was coming to say, when some idiot crowned me.'

'You? Why should *you* help me?'

'Because of Sarah. If we get Lupton back, we may get *her* back. Or at least, he may be able to tell us what happened to her.'

Yates was telling the truth, more or less. What he *didn't* say was *why* he was keen to get Lupton back. He simply wanted the chance to throttle a few answers out of him.

Barnes was still frightened. 'How do I know this isn't some kind of trick?'

'Oh, for Pete's sake,' said Yates exasperatedly. 'Of course it isn't. Now, just you untie me and we'll say no more about my bump on the head.' There was real authority in Yates' voice. Barnes bent over and started undoing the knots.

Crouched in his cupboard, Tommy sat peering into the crystal. He *wanted* to find Yates and ask his advice. But suppose Yates said he must give up the crystal. He heard voices in the corridor outside. He opened his cupboard a crack to listen. Yates – and Barnes was with him. Strange that. They'd never been friends . . .

'We'll meet in the cellar then,' Yates was saying. 'Half an hour's time O.K.?'

'I suppose so,' replied Barnes gloomily. 'It *may* do some good. I haven't had a moment's peace since Lupton vanished . . .'

The voices faded away down the corridor. Tommy frowned. He was grappling with his foggy memories of a few days ago, before the miraculous change came over him. *Everything* had been cloudy then. Sarah had said something about the cellar – and about Lupton in the cellar. Something bad had happened, and Lupton and Sarah had gone away. Now it was going to happen again. Tommy came to a decision. 'Cho-Je. I'll tell Cho-Je . . .'

He put the crystal back in its hiding place and went out.

*   *   *   *   *

Lupton and the Spider Council were in hiding, deep in the heart of the Spider Citadel. In the tunnels above them, the battle still raged. Their guards were being killed one by one. But, as yet, this secret inner room had not been found. If they could remain undiscovered for just a little longer, they might yet snatch victory from near-defeat.

Lupton watched as the Spider Council crouched in a semi-circle. They seemed rapt with concentration. He turned to his Spider. 'What is happening?'

'Contact has been re-established – the path is open.'

'And where is this contact?'

'In the place you yourself first opened,' replied one of the other Spiders.

Lupton's eyes lit up. 'The monastery? Then the group must be operating again. You'd better be careful. They're weak. They may not be trustworthy'.

'Then our approach shall be secret. Begin.'

98

The Spider Council set up a low humming. One of the Spiders moved to the centre of the circle. It glowed, and then disappeared. Another Spider moved forward to take its place.

Yates sat round the mandala in the monastery cellar, chanting with the others, and wondered what the devil he was doing. They'd been at it for what seemed ages now, and still nothing was happening. True, the unearthly glow had appeared around the mandala. But after that, nothing: no Lupton, no spiders, and above all, no Sarah. Yates began to feel that he must be as mad as the rest of this potty little group of would-be supermen . . .

(A spider materialised unseen, *not* on the mandala but in the darkness outside the circle. It scuttled away into a corner. Another and another followed it . . .)

In Cho-Je's room Tommy was finishing his story. 'So I thought I'd better come and make a clean breast of it all. I'm only sorry about not coming before.'

Cho-Je shook his head. 'Dear me, these foolish fellows. I really should have believed the Doctor, eh?' He jumped nimbly to his feet.

'Don't you think we should tell K'anpo?'

'Indeed we *shall* tell the Abbot – when we know what to tell him! Now, Tommy, you go and get this crystal, while I go to the cellar and see what these naughty fellows are about. Off you go.'

Tommy was about to obey when something struck him. 'You don't seem very surprised about the way I've changed.'

Cho-Je chuckled. 'When everything is new, how can anything be a surprise? Now go.'

Baffled, but somehow reassured, Tommy followed him from the room.

Unaware that they were getting some rather spectacular

results, the little group in the cellar continued chanting. Suddenly Yates became aware that the cellar door was opening. Cho-Je was standing at the top of the steps. 'That's torn it,' he thought ruefully. 'Not that we were getting anywhere.' It was the first time he had ever seen Cho-Je angry. The little monk was literally hopping with rage.

'You must stop,' Cho-Je spluttered. 'You are the most misguided of men! Did I not warn you?'

Suddenly a giant Spider appeared, swinging on a strand of its web through the air towards Cho-Je. Cho-Je raised his hands in disquiet, and began an Incantation of Banishment. But it was too late. A crackling finger of flame shot from the Spider's body and the frail little monk crumpled to the ground.

Appalled, Yates leaped to his feet and made for the steps. Another Spider sprang from the darkness and blasted him down.

Barnes, Moss, Keaver and Lands also jumped to their feet. From the dark corners of the cellar, the giant Spiders moved in to surround them. An icy voice ordered: 'Turn your backs.'

Minutes later, everything was quiet. The bodies of Mike Yates and Cho-Je lay on the steps.

A sudden groaning, wheezing noise filled the air, and a blue police box materialised in the middle of the cellar. The TARDIS door opened, and Sarah and the Doctor stepped out.

The Doctor looked round him in some surprise. 'Well, how very – ' He broke off as he saw the two bodies on the steps. He ran across to them, Sarah close behind.

The Doctor examined first Mike and then Cho-Je. 'At least they're not dead . . .' he said.

Four men came out of the dark cellar corners and marched towards them : Barnes, Moss, Keaver and Lands – the remaining members of Lupton's group. 'Now, then,' said the Doctor thoughtfully, 'what have you chaps been up to, eh?'

The four men made no reply. Instead, acting as one, they extended their hands in a curious pointing gesture.

With a thrill of horror, the Doctor realised the Spiders had reached earth before them. And they had found new servants . . .

11

The Battle with the Spiders

The Doctor's mind was working at tremendous speed. After so many dangers on Metebelis – to come back to this! He looked keenly at the four men. If he jumped the middle two – no, it was no good. The other two would attack him, and after that, all four would finish him off. And Sarah too . . . The Doctor glanced at her. Her face was set, showing no sign of fear.

The cellar door crashed open and Tommy came hurtling down the steps. He crashed into the four men like a human cannon ball, sending them reeling all over the cellar. 'Doctor, Sarah, quickly,' he yelled, 'up the stairs.'

They ran past him and Tommy backed away after them, his face turned towards the four men, who were now picking themselves up. Barnes, the first to recover, sent a blast of energy crackling towards Tommy, who took it fairly in the chest. But he did not fall. He winced a little, and then backed slowly up the stairs. He jumped through the door at the top, slammed it and locked it behind him.

'No,' gasped Sarah. 'What about Mike and Cho-Je?'

'They'll be out cold for quite a while yet,' said the Doctor. 'While they're unconscious they'll be safe.'

An angry banging came from inside the cellar. 'We'd better get a move on,' said Tommy. 'That door won't hold four men for long. Would you come with me, please?' he added politely. 'The Abbot is waiting to see you.'

The Doctor and Sarah looked at him in amazement. Now the excitement was over, they had time to realise that this was a very different Tommy.

'What happened to you?' asked Sarah, as they ran along the corridor.

'No idea,' said Tommy. 'Don't understand it myself.'

'But you're just like everyone else!'

Tommy grinned. 'I sincerely hope not,' he said, and held open the door to the Abbot's room.

The big room was almost completely bare except for a few scattered rugs and a Tibetan prayer-wheel. A carved wooden chair stood in the middle of the polished floor. In it sat a very old man wearing the robes of a Tibetan Abbot. His eyes were closed, either in sleep or in meditation. Behind him, in the corner, was a little shrine, candles and incense burning before it.

'This is the Doctor, Rinpoche' said Tommy softly.

The old man opened his eyes. 'I know. You are welcome'.

'And this is my friend Sarah Jane Smith,' Tommy added.

The Abbot gave Sarah one of the warmest, kindest smiles she had ever seen. 'It is kind of you to come and visit an old man.'

'Forgive me, Master,' said the Doctor, dropping instinctively into Tibetan. 'I come before you with my hands empty of gifts. Alas, I have no cotton scarf to offer you.'

In the same tongue the old man answered, 'Such a ceremonial gift is merely the symbol of friendship. We have no need of symbols, you and I.'

The Doctor looked at him curiously. The Abbot seemed to be implying that they were old friends. Yet, to the best of the Doctor's recollection, he had never seen K'anpo before. Of course, during a very long life, and several different incarnations, the Doctor had met a great number of people. Perhaps it would come back to him.

'I'd better keep watch,' said Tommy. 'They'll be out of that cellar soon.'

K'anpo Rinpoche closed his eyes momentarily. Yet somehow he seemed to be *looking*. He opened them again.

'As yet they have not managed it,' he said placidly, 'but they will – very soon.'

Tommy slipped out of the room and the old Abbot turned to the Doctor. 'Now, Doctor, I think you have a story to tell me.'

'Somehow I have a feeling you already know most of it. It concerns a certain blue crystal that I found . . .'

'Found?' interrupted the old man gently.

The Doctor rubbed his chin. Sarah could see that he was rather taken aback. 'Well, perhaps "stole" *would* be a better word.' The Doctor looked at the old man sharply. 'Forgive me – but *have* we met before?'

K'anpo smiled benignly. 'The recognition of friends is not always easy. Tell me about the crystal that you – stole.'

The Doctor cleared his throat. 'Ah, well, yes . . . It didn't occur to me that I *was* stealing it of course – not at the time . . .'

As the Doctor launched into his narrative, Sarah sat back unnoticed watching the calm face of K'anpo Rinpoche. There was something very strange, very powerful, about this frail old man. Sarah could see that the Doctor had noticed it too.

With a wrenching and tearing noise, the cellar door burst open at last, the iron lock torn clean from the wood. Barnes, Moss, Keaver and Lands all tumbled out into the corridor on top of one another. Barnes assumed control. 'We must spread out and search for them. They won't have gone far.'

Little Moss shook his head vigorously. He'd had enough. 'I'm leaving. I don't want anything more to do with it.' He had time to take only a single step before something inside his head caught and twisted at his mind. Moss screamed, his hands clawing at his temples. 'No, no, please stop it. I'll do anything. Please, make it stop!'

The pain died, and the icy voice in his head said, 'You will obey me?'

Moss sobbed, 'Yes, yes, anything.'

The four men stood looking at each other. The taciturn Keaver said slowly, 'What are we supposed to *do*?'

'I can see a stone,' said Lands, 'a blue stone . . .'

'Yes – you must find the crystal,' said the icy voice of a Spider. 'Concentrate. All concentrate.'

After a moment Barnes said, 'Yes, I can see it too. It's that way.'

The little group of men moved slowly but surely towards the Abbot's room.

'The crystal must be more important than I ever realised,' concluded the Doctor. 'Obviously the Spiders need it very badly. I think it's the last piece in the jigsaw of their power.'

'Then perhaps they should have it,' said the Abbot.

The Doctor knew that the suggestion was made only to test his response. 'Never. I've seen how they rule on Metebelis Three. Something tells me that if they get their hands on the crystal, nothing will stop them from taking over the Earth.'

'Or even the Universe,' said Sarah suddenly. Both men looked at her. Her eyes were wide, her expression intent. Again, the Doctor thought that there had been something strained about Sarah ever since their reunion in the Spiders' Citadel. It was as if, in some way, the Spiders had left their mark on her. As soon as all this was over, he'd see that she took a very long rest. He turned back to the Abbot.

'As Sarah says, they may even want to take over the Universe. I only wish I knew where the crystal was now. Sarah tells me that Lupton didn't succeed in taking it to Metebelis Three after all.'

K'anpo Rinpoche opened his hands, which had been folded on his lap. In his palm nestled the blue crystal.

'Tommy brought it to me,' he said simply. The Doctor smiled.

'Yes, of course. I should have known the moment I saw the change in him. The crystal cleared his mind. Thank Heavens it's safe.'

'Give it to *me*,' said Sarah suddenly.

The Doctor looked at her astonished. 'Sarah, what's the matter?'

When Sarah spoke next, it was in the voice of the Queen Spider. 'Give *me* the crystal. I must have it. I must have it . . .'

She went to snatch the crystal, but the Doctor stepped in front of her. Instantly Sarah's hand came up in a pointing gesture, and a blast of mental energy sent the Doctor reeling back. Sarah stepped forward to snatch the crystal from the Abbot's lap.

The old man raised a warning hand. 'Stay, I command you!'

Sarah stopped. The power which controlled her mind was blocked by the Abbot's will.

Still wincing from the attack, the Doctor stepped forward. 'Sarah, listen to me . . .'

K'anpo shook his head. 'She cannot hear you, Doctor. See!' The shape of the Queen Spider had materialised on Sarah's back.

'Give me the crystal, old man, or you die!' continued Sarah in the Spider's cruel voice.

'Struggle against the Spider, Sarah,' said the Doctor fiercely. 'Fight it!'

Sarah spoke again in the Spider's voice. 'I am the Queen! Obey me! Give me the crystal!'

'No,' said the Abbot gently. 'You are *Sarah*. Remember that you are *Sarah*.'

The struggle between Sarah's true self and the controlling Spider Queen locked her lips. She could make only guttural choking sounds.

'Look into the crystal,' said the Doctor suddenly. 'Look into its blue light and *see* that you are free.'

106

Sarah swayed to and fro in great distress. The voice from her lips fluctuated, sometimes coming out as her own voice, sometimes as that of the Spider Queen. 'I am the Queen. No, no, I am Sarah. I am free. I am the Queen, the Queen must live . . . '

The Doctor and K'anpo leaned over her trying desperately to help. 'Concentrate on the crystal, Sarah,' repeated the Doctor.

'You . . . are . . . free,' urged K'anpo. 'You do not have to be dominated. Look and see that you are free.'

Sarah gazed into the crystal. Slowly, she felt her mind coming back under her own control.

The Queen Spider on Sarah's back twitched and fell on the floor. Having been defeated by her host at last, she gave a high piercing cry, her body twisted and writhed, then withered away to nothing. Sarah sobbed in relief, and fell forward into the Doctor's arms.

Outside the Abbot's door Tommy heard footsteps moving stealthily towards him. Barnes and his friends crept round the corner. They moved as one, like Zombies. They came to a halt when they saw Tommy, and then moved forward menacingly.

'Get out of our way, Tommy,' said Barnes.

Tommy shook his head. 'You can't go in there.'

Barnes raised his hand and pointed. There was a line of fire, the crackle of a mental-energy attack caused Tommy to stumble back, but he remained on his feet.

'Rush him!' ordered Barnes, and all four men ran at Tommy at once. They soon discovered their mistake. One by one, Tommy plucked them off, and hurled them down the corridor. Barnes was the last to be thrown aside. He fell awkwardly, sliding down the wall.

'Sorry, Mr. Barnes,' said Tommy gently. 'You can't go in there.'

Barnes staggered to his feet. 'Kill him,' he ordered viciously. All four men pointed at Tommy and blasted him with the power imparted by the Spiders. Tommy reeled and staggered, gripping the door frame for support. But at the end of the attack he was still on his feet, and still blocking the doorway with his massive body.

Barnes and the others fell back, gasping and drained. Inside their heads, the Spiders' voices conferred. 'We need more power.'

'I agree! We need more power.'

'Concentrate, Sisters.'

'Concentrate . . .'

Barnes and the others gathered in a circle, and closed their eyes. A low humming filled the hallway. Tommy looked on, and braced himself for the next attack. He was determined that they should never enter that room while he was alive to stop them.

Sarah sobbed. 'I'm sorry, Doctor.'

'Don't be. You did very well, Sarah. You freed yourself.'

Sarah shuddered. 'But I *let* that creature take me over.'

K'anpo said gently, 'We are all apt to surrender ourself to domination. Not all spiders are on the back.'

Suddenly the Doctor swung round on K'anpo. 'Of course. I know who you are now.'

'You were always a little slow on the uptake, my boy.'

The Doctor and K'anpo clasped hands, like old friends meeting after long years of separation.

'It's been a long time,' said the Doctor affectionately.

Sarah looked from one to the other of them. 'Then you two *have* met before?'

The Doctor said, 'He was my teacher, my guru, if you like. You've heard me speak of him.'

Sarah said, 'So you're a Time Lord too?'

K'anpo nodded. 'But the discipline they imposed was not for me.'

'Or me,' said the Doctor. 'We both had to get away.'

'The Doctor, er, borrowed a TARDIS and set off on

his wanderings. And I regenerated and came here to Earth.'

'Regenerated?' said Sarah weakly.

'When a Time Lord's body wears out,' explained the Doctor, 'it can regenerate – become new.'

Sarah shook her head, baffled. A thought struck her. 'What about Cho-Je? Is he a Time Lord, too?'

K'anpo smiled. 'Cho-Je is merely a projection. You might say he was my other self.'

Mike Yates recovered consciousness, to see Cho-Je leaning over him, apparently none the worse. 'Come, Mr. Yates,' said the little monk. 'There is no time to lose.' Groggily, Mike got to his feet and followed Cho-Je out of the cellar.

Outside the Abbot's door, Barnes and the others still stood in a circle. Tommy watched and waited, bracing himself for the final ordeal.

In his room, K'anpo stood up. 'I have enjoyed our reunion, Doctor. But now the moment approaches.'

'What moment?' asked Sarah.

'The moment of death,' said the old man placidly. 'The moment I have been waiting for. You know what to do, Doctor?'

Sarah had never seen the Doctor so uncertain. 'No,' he said, 'I'm not sure . . .'

'I think you do know, my son,' said the old man softly. 'What is it that you most fear?'

The Doctor looked at him despairingly. 'There is *no* other way?'

'None.'

The Doctor heaved a sigh, seeming to accept some fate that was inevitable, but far from pleasant. 'Very well. Give me the crystal.'

Sarah looked from one to the other in anguish. 'What

is *happening*, Doctor? What are you planning to do?'

The Doctor looked at her in surprise. 'The only thing I can do. I started all this trouble by taking the crystal. Now I must set things right by returning it to the cave of the Great One.'

Outside, the little group ceased their concentration. Barnes spoke but it was the voice of his Spider that came from his lips. 'Enough. The power is sufficient.' As they swung round on Tommy, Cho-Je and Yates came along the corridor. Barnes shouted 'Now!'

A tremendous web of energy crackled around the four men. It flung Tommy, Yates and Cho-Je to one side like thistledown. Barnes and the others rushed into the Abbot's room.

Facing them were Sarah, the Doctor, and K'anpo. The Doctor held the crystal in his hand. K'anpo jumped in front of the Doctor as if to protect the crystal with his frail body. The energy web crackled, K'anpo fell – and the Doctor disappeared, winking out of existence..

The four men froze for a moment. Then Barnes said in his Spider's voice, 'He is in the cellar – come!'

They rushed from the room. Sarah knelt by K'anpo's body. He seemed completely lifeless.

Teleported by the force of the old Time Lord's will, the Doctor found himself standing beside the TARDIS, crystal in hand. He produced the TARDIS key, opened the door and disappeared inside. Seconds later, the dematerialisation began. Barnes and the others rushed into the cellar, just in time to see the TARDIS vanish. The Doctor was on his way to confront his last enemy.

12

The Last Enemy

The Doctor stepped from the TARDIS and looked cautiously about him. As he had expected, he had materialised in the heart of the Spider Citadel, not far from the cave of the Great One. He was at the junction of four tunnels. He could see by the concentration of blue crystals glowing in the walls that he was in the right area. But he was still unsure of the right way to go. All the tunnels looked exactly alike.

Suddenly Arak and Tuar came along the tunnel to his left, both with swords in their hands. He greeted them with pleasure. 'Your attack was a success then?'

Arak nodded. 'Thanks to you, Doctor.' There was no joy in Arak's voice. The Doctor assumed that he was exhausted from the fighting.

'Now I need your help, my friends,' he said. 'I need to go to the Cave of the Crystal.'

Tuar said flatly, 'If you go into the cave you will die. The power of the crystals is so concentrated that it will kill you.'

'I have to go. Will you show me the way?'

Arak nodded. 'Come, Doctor.'

They led the Doctor along an endless maze of tunnels, until at last they came to a blank wall. Arak touched his palm to it and immediately a stone slid back, revealing a small archway. Arak stepped back. 'Through there, Doctor.' The Doctor stepped through, and found himself facing Lupton and the web which held the full

Council of the Spiders. He turned to run, but Arak and Tuar were behind him with drawn swords.

The Doctor sighed. 'The rebellion failed then?' Arak and Tuar did not speak.

One of the Spiders, evidently the new Queen, answered him. 'No, Doctor, it succeeded,' she said venomously. The rest of the mountain is in the hands of the rebels you stirred up against us. But here, in the heart of the mountain, close to the Cave of Crystal, the protection you gave them was weakened. These two were rash. They ventured too far, and we captured their minds.'

Another Spider joined in. 'We kept them alive to be sure of trapping you. We felt sure you would return. Now we have the crystal and they will die. All the rebels will die, and Metebelis will be ours again. Then Earth, then any planet we choose to take!'

The new Queen said eagerly, 'We know you have the crystal. We can feel it. Give it to us.'

Slowly the Doctor took the crystal from his pocket. He held it high. A hum of excitement rose from the Council. The Doctor's voice cut through it. 'I came back here at the express command of the Great One. I came to return the crystal to her. Think well. We are close to her cave. Perhaps she reads your thoughts. Is there anyone here who would dare to take the crystal from me?'

There was a moment's silence. Then Lupton stepped forward. 'I would dare.' He turned to address the Council. 'Give the crystal to this mad Great One of yours and she'll have power to destroy the lot of us. I will take it.'

He stepped forward to reach out for the crystal. The Queen Spider said, 'Lupton!' The will of the united Spider Council held Lupton in a grip of iron. He froze, statue-like. His fingers were inches from the crystal.

He spoke with enormous effort. 'But why? All we planned, all we dreamed of, is there in the palm of his hand. The recapture of Metebelis, the conquest of the Earth, the conquest of a thousand planets.' Lupton babbled on, but his voice was drowned by the chanting of the Council.

'The Great One is all seeing.'

'The Great One is all knowing.'

'The Great One is all powerful.'

The Spider Queen said, 'You have beaten us, Doctor. It is good that you will die. Go!'

The Doctor turned. Arak and Tuar stood aside. The Doctor looked at them sadly and walked through the arch.

Once he was gone the Spiders loosed the constraint of their will, and Lupton found he could move again. He swung round on the Council, shaking with fury. 'You fools! Stupid, cowardly, superstitious fools!'

Fiercely the Queen said 'Be silent, Lupton.'

Lupton should have seen that his usefulness, never very great, was now over. His life hung by a thread as fine as a Spider's web. Lost to all sense of self-preservation, he ranted on. 'To think I've lost my chance of power, my chance to rule the whole rotten stinking world.' He was almost weeping with rage. 'And all because of a lot of Spiders.'

A shudder of horror went round the Council at the forbidden word. Lupton saw it, and was glad.

'Yes, Spiders! Spiders I'd crush underfoot on Earth without a second thought.'

Lupton actually raised a foot to stamp on the Spider Queen. At once energy-blasts flashed forth from every member of the Council. All the hatred and bitterness of their defeat was poured out upon him. The crackle of the web of power lifted his body and held it, screaming and glowing and twisting in the air. Then it dropped to the ground, a shattered lump.

The Queen spoke. 'This two-legs can do us a last service, my sisters. Let us feast on our favourite food once more before the end.'

The Spider Council began to close in on Lupton's body.

*   *   *   *   *

Tommy recovered consciousness to see Cho-Je bending over him. 'You are well, Tommy. That is good.' Cho-Je moved across to Yates. He knelt beside him, his face grave. Tommy struggled over to join him.

'I think he's dead, Cho-Je.'

'Not yet. Let us take him to K'anpo Rinpoche. He will heal him.' Together they managed to manhandle Yates' inert body into the Abbot's room. K'anpo was sitting up in his chair, helped there by Sarah.

He looked weak and shaken, but his eyes were bright and alert. Cho-Je and Tommy carried Yates across to the chair and propped him up, resting his head in the old Abbot's lap. 'Please, can't you help him?' asked Sarah.

K'anpo seemed to brace himself for one final effort. He laid his hands on Yates' forehead, and closed his eyes in concentration. Then he opened them, smiling. After a moment Yates too opened his eyes and struggled to sit up. 'Hullo, Sarah Jane,' he said weakly.

'His courage and compassion protected him,' said the Abbot. 'You too, my son,' he added, turning to Tommy. 'Your mind was as new and fresh as a child's! Innocence was your shield. That is why the evil of the Spiders' minds could not destroy you.'

Yates struggled to his feet and stretched.

'We thought you'd had it,' said Sarah.

He grinned. 'Not this time – I feel fine now.'

Suddenly Tommy gave a cry of alarm. 'K'anpo!'

The old man lay back in his chair, shaking and gasping for breath. He smiled weakly at them. 'I'm very much afraid this old body has "had it" as you say.' He produced the newly-learned colloquialism with evident pride.

Sarah felt herself starting to cry. 'Oh no, you can't die. You can't.'

The Abbot looked distressed. 'Please, do not grieve, my friends.' His head fell back. Cho-Je, who had been sitting cross-legged beside him, suddenly vanished. As they watched, the body of K'anpo began to glow with a golden light. His features blurred and swam, and then seemed to settle into those of Cho-Je. The glow faded and now Cho-Je sat in the chair, beaming at them. 'I was not dying, you see, I was merely regenerating.'

Tommy shook his head in amazement. 'Cho-Je – '

Cho-Je shook his head and held up a warning finger. 'No, no. I *was* Cho-Je, I am now K'anpo. Or, if you prefer, I am both!'

Sarah said shakily, 'Look, whoever, whichever, you are, I'm glad you're all right again. But please can you tell us what's happening to the Doctor? Is he still in the monastery?'

Cho-Je shook his head. 'I fear by now he is back on Metebelis Three.'

'When will he come back?'

Cho-Je's face was grave. He took Sarah's hand. 'I am sorry to have to tell you, my dear young lady, that it is highly unlikely that you, or anyone else, will ever see the Doctor again.'

*   *   *   *   *

The Doctor wandered through the glowing blue tunnels with no very clear idea where he was going. He simply took the paths leading downwards, or those where the blue glow was brightest. He plodded on and on with the crystal clutched in his hand. He seemed to be in a kind of endless nightmare. At last he came to a tunnel he knew. At the end of it he saw the deep blue glow of the Cave of Crystal. The Doctor paused for a moment, as if to brace himself. Then he moved on down the tunnel.

This time when he came to the cave he did not stop but walked straight on into its blue glow. At once the sweet, mad voice of the Great One sounded in his ears. 'Stop! Have you brought me the crystal?'

Wearily the Doctor said 'If I had not, why should I have returned?'

'Very well. Advance.'

The Doctor walked on into the blue haze. As he went on, it seemed to clear. He looked around him in awe. He was in a vast blue cave, the size of a cathedral. The walls shimmered and glowed with uncanny light. The crystal in his hand picked them up, and returned the glow. At the far end of the cave was a complicated lattice-work, a sort of super-web made entirely from blue crystal. At the centre of it sat the most enormous Spider the Doctor had ever seen, larger by a hundred times than her sisters who ruled the planet. He was looking at the Great One. The last wonder he would ever see.

'Why have you come?' she asked. 'Why have you destroyed yourself?'

'I want to make you see that what you plan to do is wrong.'

'I am the Great One. I can do no wrong.'

'I will bargain with you. Take the crystal and let the humans live in peace – here and on Earth.'

Mad laughter rang through the Crystal Cave. 'What do you think I care for the plans of my subjects? Earth is nothing to me. Give me the crystal!'

Even in such an extreme situation, the Doctor's scientific curiosity was still strong. It had been a dominant characteristic all his life and it did not abandon him at the end. 'First, tell me why you need the crystal so?'

'You see this web? It reproduces the patterns of my brain. One perfect crystal is missing from the design. The crystal which you stole! It is unique, and irreplaceable.'

The immense concentration of the blue crystal vibrations was sapping the Doctor's mind and destroying his body. He knew he could not last much longer. 'When the crystal web is complete – what then?' he asked weakly.

The Great One's voice was exultant. 'My every thought will resonate within the web. My mind will grow and grow in power – forever!'

'Don't you see?' shouted the Doctor desperately. 'You've built a positive feedback circuit. You're trying to increase your mental powers to infinity!'

'Exactly. I shall be the Ruler of the entire Universe.'

'Listen to me please,' begged the Doctor. 'I haven't

very much time. If you complete that circuit, the energy will build up and up until you can no longer contain it. You will literally destroy yourself. You will explode your mind!'

'You waste the little time that is left to you,' said the Great One disdainfully. 'I will grant you one last favour. You may watch the completion of my triumph while you die.'

The blue crystal was plucked from the Doctor's hand. It floated gently across the cave and filled the one remaining gap in the crystal web which had waited for it so long. The Great One gave a shriek of triumph. 'I am complete. Now I am total power. All praise to the Great One!'

The Doctor, now very weak, watched helplessly as his prophetic warning came true. The crystal web began to glow, brighter and brighter. The walls of the Crystal Cave seemed to be on fire. The shrieks of the Great One echoed around the Cave. 'ALL PRAISE TO THE GREAT ONE. ALL PRAISE TO ME. ON YOUR KNEES, MORTALS. BOW DOWN BEFORE ME PLANETS. BOW DOWN O STARS. BOW DOWN O GALAXIES, AND WORSHIP THE GREAT ONE, THE *ME* THE GREAT ALL-POWERFUL *ME*!'

Suddenly a scream of pain filled the cave. 'I AM HURT. I AM BURNING, MY BRAIN IS ON FIRE. HELP ME!'

The crystal web was white hot now, and the body of the Great One was incandescent, as she writhed and twisted in agony. The Doctor knew there was no hope for him now. He had been too long in the cave. He decided that he did not particularly want to spend whatever time was left to him in watching the Great One die. He turned and stumbled away.

The final throes of the Great One were the death knell of all the Giant Spiders of Metebelis Three. Their minds linked in some mystic way to hers, they died as she died.

In the hidden Council Chamber Arak and Tuar suddenly felt themselves wake up. All around them Spiders were twisting and dying. 'We are free,' said Arak. 'Come, my brother.' They turned and ran from the chamber. The whole mountain was shaking now as if in an earthquake. At last, they gained the open air and ran down the mountainside to where their followers stood waiting. Arak, his brother, and their little army looked on from a safe distance as the mountain of blue crystals exploded in a mass of flames. When it was over at last, they turned and made their way back to the villages. Tomorrow would indeed be a new dawn for Metebelis Three. The dawn of freedom.

In the cellar of the monastery, Barnes and his group waited for instructions which never came. Instead, Spiders appeared one by one upon their backs, dropped to the ground and withered away to nothingness. The four men looked at each other in sudden horror and disgust. Barnes began to sob . . .

In the heart of the exploding mountain, the Doctor ran alone along endless tunnels. At last he saw the one thing he was looking for – the solid blue shape of the TARDIS. Fearful that it might be a mirage, he gathered the last remnants of his strength and stumbled towards it.

Epilogue

An End and a Beginning

Sarah Jane Smith stood and looked round the Doctor's laboratory. You could tell he wasn't there, she thought, by the fact that the place was so abnormally tidy : all the tangles of equipment cleared away, laboratory benches bare and polished stools ranged neatly along the wall. Perhaps the most noticeable change of all was the empty space in the corner where the TARDIS usually stood. One of the Doctor's old cloaks hung from the peg behind the door. Sarah held it to her cheek for a moment, then turned away.

Beside her the Brigadier cleared his throat. 'Like to keep the place standing by, you know. Just in case the old fellow turns up to use it.'

Sarah said 'He's been gone for over three weeks now.'

'That's nothing,' said the Brigadier stoutly. 'After the first time I met him, we didn't meet again for some years. And then he turned up with a completely different face.' The Brigadier still sounded a little aggrieved.

'He *knew* if he went back there he'd destroy himself,' Sarah went on bleakly. 'We might as well face it, Brigadier, we'll never see him again.'

The Brigadier made no comment. He didn't really know what had happened to the Doctor and Sarah on Metebelis Three, and didn't see much point in finding out. He'd paid a lightning visit to the monastery, when it was all over, and found Yates and Sarah badly shaken and four chaps with complete nervous breakdowns who'd had to be carted off in ambulances. A man called Lupton was missing. There was also some story about the Abbot disappearing, but since no one seemed very sure if he'd ever been there in the first place, the Brigadier proposed to let that one strictly alone. Oh yes, and there was that fellow Tommy. Sarah had made the Brigadier promise to use his influence to get him a place at University.

Remembering Sarah's feelings, the Brigadier made another valiant effort to console her. 'Thing is, Miss Smith, the Doctor's a very resilient chap – I remember once . . .'

A wheezing, groaning sound filled the laboratory. The TARDIS began to materialise in its usual corner. Once it was solidly there, the Doctor staggered out and collapsed at their feet.

Sarah and the Brigadier made the transition from joy to sorrow in an instant. The Doctor looked – the only word was deathly. Like the ghost of his former self. It seemed as if the very fabric of his body had been eroded away. He sat up and looked at them with an apologetic grin. 'Sorry to be so long . . . lost in the Time Vortex. TARDIS brought me home.' He gave the TARDIS an affectionate pat, and fell back on the floor. Sarah kneeled beside him, cradling his head in her lap. She began to sob gently, and a tear splashed on to the end of the Doctor's nose. His eyes flickered open. 'Tears, Sarah Jane? You mustn't cry. Remember, while there's life there's . . .' The Doctor's eyes closed again and his head fell back.

The Brigadier said quickly, 'I'll get the M.O. May still be something . . .' He made for the phone.

'Too late, Brigadier. He's dead.'

'Oh no!' said a voice behind her. 'He is not dead, my dear young lady.'

Sarah turned and saw Cho-Je. She jumped to her feet, noticing with no feeling of surprise that he was sitting cross-legged in mid-air about three feet above the ground.

'Oh dear,' she said to no one in particular. 'I don't think I can take much more.'

The Brigadier looked at Cho-Je severely, as if wondering how he'd slipped into the building without a pass. 'Won't you introduce me to your friend, Miss Smith?'

Sarah said helplessly, 'Well, it's Cho-Je. That is, it looks like Cho-Je but it's really K'anpo Rinpoche – I think.'

'Thank you,' said the Brigadier. 'That makes everything quite clear.'

Sarah looked up at Cho-Je and said, 'You're *sure* he isn't dead?'

Cho-Je nodded. 'All the cells of his body have been devastated by the Metebelis crystals. But remember, he *is* a Time Lord. If I give the process a little – ah – a little push, so to speak, the cells will regenerate. He will be a new man!'

'Literally?' asked the Brigadier, with a certain amount of foreboding.

Cho-Je smiled. 'Well of course he is bound to look different.'

The Brigadier sighed. 'Not again.'

And there was more to come. Cho-Je said, 'The change will shake up the brain cells a little. You may find him rather erratic at first. But he'll settle down.'

Sarah looked worriedly at the Doctor as he lay on the floor. 'And when is all this going to happen?'

Cho-Je chuckled. 'Well, there's no time like the present is there? Goodbye – look after him.' And he faded away as silently as he had appeared.

'Now wait a moment,' said the Brigadier firmly. His voice tailed off as he realised he was addressing empty space.

'Brigadier, look!' said Sarah. 'It's starting.'

A golden glow was appearing round the Doctor's body. Even as they watched, the features began to blur and change. 'Well bless my soul,' said the Brigadier. 'Here we go again!'

ROMANCE

0352   Star

	Unity Hall	
396695	**LOVING IN MY FASHION**	60p
39627X	**VALLEY OF THE CHILDREN**	60p
	Daisy Thomson	
395001	**BE MY LOVE**	60p*
398698	**JOURNEY TO LOVE**	50p*
397063	**PORTRAIT OF MY LOVE**	60p*
397055	**PRELUDE TO LOVE**	60p*
398701	**WOMAN IN LOVE**	50p*
395451	**A TRUCE FOR LOVE**	60p*
397195	**TO LOVE AND HONOUR**	60p*
398760	**SUMMONS TO LOVE**	60p*
395206	**HELLO MY LOVE**	60p*

0426   Tandem

	Barbara Michaels	
178868	**AMMIE COME HOME**	60p

TARGET STORY BOOKS

'Doctor Who'

† For sale in Britain and Ireland only.
* Not for sale in Canada.
♦ Film & T.V. tie-ins.

TARGET STORY BOOKS

'Doctor Who'

200020	DOCTOR WHO DISCOVERS PREHISTORIC ANIMALS	(NF)	(illus)	75p
200039	DOCTOR WHO DISCOVERS SPACE TRAVEL	(NF)	(illus)	75p
200047	DOCTOR WHO DISCOVERS STRANGE AND MYSTERIOUS CREATURES	(NF)	(illus)	75p
20008X	DOCTOR WHO DISCOVERS THE STORY OF EARLY MAN	(NF)	(illus)	75p
200136	DOCTOR WHO DISCOVERS THE CONQUERORS	(NF)	(illus)	75p

Ian Marter
116313 DOCTOR WHO AND THE ARK IN SPACE   50p

Terrance Dicks
116747 DOCTOR WHO AND THE BRAIN OF MORBIUS   50p*

Terrance Dicks
110250 DOCTOR WHO AND THE CARNIVAL OF MONSTERS   50p

Malcolm Hulke
11471X DOCTOR WHO AND THE CAVE MONSTERS   60p

Terrance Dicks
117034 DOCTOR WHO AND THE CLAWS OF AXOS   50p*

David Whitaker
113160 DOCTOR WHO AND THE CRUSADERS   (illus) 60p

Brian Hayles
114981 DOCTOR WHO AND THE CURSE OF PELADON   60p

Gerry Davis
114639 DOCTOR WHO AND THE CYBERMEN   60p

Barry Letts
113322 DOCTOR WHO AND THE DAEMONS   (illus) 40p

David Whitaker
101103 DOCTOR WHO AND THE DALEKS   60p

Terrance Dicks
11244X DOCTOR WHO AND THE DALEK INVASION OF EARTH   60p

Terrance Dicks
119657 DOCTOR WHO AND THE DEADLY ASSASSIN   60p

Terrance Dicks
200063 DOCTOR WHO AND THE FACE OF EVIL   60p

Terrance Dicks
112601 DOCTOR WHO AND THE GENESIS OF THE DALEKS   60p

TARGET STORY BOOKS

Adventure

	Gordon Boshell	
113918	**THE BLACK MERCEDES**	60p
114043	**THE MILLION POUND RANSOM**	60p
117468	**THE MENDIP MONEY-MAKERS**	60p

Animal Stories

	Molly Burkett			
118502	**FOXES, OWLS AND ALL**	(NF)	(illus)	70p
111567	**THAT MAD, BAD BADGER . . .**	(NF)	(illus)	35p
	Constance Taber Colby			
109899	**A SKUNK IN THE FAMILY**	(NF)	(illus)	45p
	I. J. Edmonds			
20011X	**LASSIE: THE WILD MOUNTAIN TRAIL**			60p
	G. D. Griffiths			
113675	**ABANDONED!**		(illus)	50p
	David Gross			
117549	**THE BADGERS OF BADGER HILL**		(illus)	50p
	Michael Maguire			
118774	**MYLOR, THE MOST POWERFUL HORSE IN THE WORLD**		(illus)	60p
	Joyce Stranger			
11017X	**THE SECRET HERDS**		(illus)	45p
110099	**THE HARE AT DARK HOLLOW**		(illus)	40p

Mystery And Suspense

	Ruth M. Arthur		
111648	**THE AUTUMN GHOSTS**	(illus)	50p
111729	**THE CANDLEMAS MYSTERY**	(illus)	45p*
	Tim Dinsdale		
105915	**THE STORY OF THE LOCH NESS MONSTER**	(illus)	50p
	Leonard Gribble		
104285	**FAMOUS HISTORICAL MYSTERIES**	(NF) (illus)	50p
	Alfred Hitchcock (Editor)		
117387	**ALFRED HITCHCOCK'S TALES OF TERROR AND SUSPENSE**		60p
	Mollie Hunter		
113756	**THE WALKING STONES**	(illus)	45p*
	Freya Littledale		
107357	**GHOSTS AND SPIRITS OF MANY LANDS**	(illus)	50p

†For sale in Britain and Ireland only.
*Not for sale in Canada.
♦ Film & T.V. tie-ins.

TARGET STORY BOOKS

Fantasy And General Fiction

	Elisabeth Beresford		
101537	**AWKWARD MAGIC**	(illus)	60p
10479X	**SEA-GREEN MAGIC**	(illus)	60p
101618	**TRAVELLING MAGIC**	(illus)	60p
	Eileen Dunlop		
119142	**ROBINSHEUGH**	(illus)	60p
	Maria Gripe		
112288	**THE GLASSBLOWER'S CHILDREN**	(illus)	45p
	Joyce Nicholson		
117891	**FREEDOM FOR PRISCILLA**		70p
	Hilary Seton		
106989	**THE HUMBLES**	(illus)	50p
109112	**THE NOEL STREATFEILD CHRISTMAS HOLIDAY BOOK**	(illus)	60p
109031	**THE NOEL STREATFEILD EASTER HOLIDAY BOOK**	(illus)	60p
105249	**THE NOEL STREATFEILD SUMMER HOLIDAY BOOK**	(illus)	50p

Humour

	Eleanor Estes		
107519	**THE WITCH FAMILY**	(illus)	50p
	Felice Holman		
11762X	**THE WITCH ON THE CORNER**	(illus)	50p
	Spike Milligan		
105672	**BADJELLY THE WITCH**	(illus)	60p
109546	**DIP THE PUPPY**	(illus)	60p
	Christine Nostlinger		
107438	**THE CUCUMBER KING**	(illus)	45p
	Mary Rogers		
119223	**A BILLION FOR BORIS**		60p

0426   Film And TV Tie-ins

	Kathleen N. Daly		
200187	**RAGGEDY ANN AND ANDY** (Colour illus)		75p ♦
	John Ryder Hall		
11826X	**SINBAD AND THE EYE OF THE TIGER**		70p* ♦
	John Lucarotti		
11535X	**OPERATION PATCH**		45p
	Pat Sandys		
119495	**THE PAPER LADS**		60p ♦
	Alison Thomas		
115511	**BENJI**		40p

†For sale in Britain and Ireland only.
*Not for sale in Canada.
♦ Film & T.V. tie-ins.

Wyndham Books are obtainable from many booksellers and newsagents. If you have any difficulty please send purchase price plus postage on the scale below to:

Wyndham Cash Sales,
PO Box 11,
Falmouth,
Cornwall

OR

Star Book Service,
G.P.O. Box 29,
Douglas,
Isle of Man,
British Isles.

While every effort is made to keep prices low, it is sometimes necessary to increase prices at short notice. Wyndham Books reserve the right to show new retail prices on covers which may differ from those advertised in the text or elsewhere.

Postage and Packing Rate
U.K.

One book 22p plus 10p per copy for each additional book ordered to a maximum charge of 82p.

B.F.P.O. & Eire

One book 22p plus 10p per copy for the next 6 books, and thereafter 4p per book.

Overseas

One book 30p plus 10p per copy for each additional book.

These charges are subject to Post Office fluctuations.